P9-BJS-679

KEEPING SECRETS

Look for these other books about
The Practically Popular Crowd:

Wanting More
Pretty Enough
Getting Smart

THE PRACTICALLY POPULAR CROWD

KEEPING SECRETS

Meg F. Schneider

AN
APPLE
PAPERBACK

SCHOLASTIC INC.
New York Toronto London Auckland Sydney

If you purchased this book without a cover, you should be aware that this book is stolen property. It was reported as "unsold and destroyed" to the publisher, and neither the author nor the publisher has received any payment for this "stripped book."

No part of this publication may be reproduced in whole or in part, or stored in a retrieval system, or transmitted in any form or by any means, electronic, mechanical, photocopying, recording, or otherwise, without written permission of the publisher. For information regarding permission, write to Scholastic Inc., 730 Broadway, New York, NY 10003.

ISBN 0-590-45477-3

Copyright © 1993 by Meg F. Schneider. All rights reserved. Published by Scholastic Inc. APPLE PAPERBACKS is a registered trademark of Scholastic Inc.

12 11 10 9 8 7 6 5 4 3 2   3 4 5 6 7 8/9

Printed in the U.S.A.   40

First Scholastic printing, January 1993

To Lisa, Vicki, and Kathy —
my own PPC

Prologue

Alexa looked out the library window and watched as David walked across the campus.

She smiled. She'd never felt this way before. It was the nicest feeling. David was so warm, and funny, and smart.

She looked down at her history text. If only that were enough.

If only he were more popular. More in demand.

Anxiously, Alexa ran a hand through her thick blonde hair.

If only a person could hide another person.

She sighed.

Star power was really like a feather.

Hers could just float away.

Alexa pressed her nose to the window. Watching.

If only they could date . . . invisibly.

1

Gina Dumont swung through the doors of Sheila's Coffee Shop and looked around. None of her friends had arrived yet. She checked the clock above the counter. Three-thirty on the nose.

Perfect. Right on time.

Gina found an empty booth and slid inside, facing the big glass window and the street. Smiling at the waitress, she ordered a Coke. She was about to settle back against the red plastic seat when she stood up and switched to the opposite side of the booth. Gina sighed and leaned back.

Her friends loved watching the street. They always said so. Why not let them?

Minutes ticked by. Gina reached into her red tote, pulled out a geography workbook, and flipped it open. Her pencil flew across the page. Romania on top. Bulgaria below. Italy the boot. Portugal the tip.

But it wasn't helping.

It was happening again.

That dreadful feeling. It was coming back.

What was the matter with her, anyway? These were her best friends. Her crowd. Her everything. So what if they were late? Often. So what if she went along with things a little?

A lot.

What *was* important was that they were friends. Friends had to give. Gina paused, her pencil hovering above the page. Or was it give in?

She couldn't quite sort out the difference. Still, she was sure there was one.

A big one, too.

Gina settled back into the booth. Calm down, she instructed herself. There was nothing to be upset about. What mattered was that everyone liked her. She smiled.

And that they stuck together.

Gina went back to work and, a moment later, Margo Warner and Priscilla Levitt breezed in.

"So sorry we're late!" Margo sang out, giving Gina's long, straight, light brown hair an affectionate tug. "We just got to talking with some kids outside school. And staring at Alexa's latest getup." Margo giggled and shook her head. "What I wouldn't give for that bod." She looked around the coffee shop. "Where's Michelle and Viv?"

"Late again," Priscilla answered a little too loudly, her hands plastered playfully over her ears. "I am so sick of hearing about Alexa's body. Who cares? She dumped us! Forget about her! We're too good for her!" She grinned sheepishly. "Aren't we? What's the Alexa Trio got over us?"

Gina shrugged. Who knew? She'd always been afraid of Alexa when they'd been friends. She was just so tough. So sure of herself. Of course, Alexa was also a miserable friend. Gina smiled softly. Proudly. Unlike herself.

Gina's eyes traveled admiringly over the jean vest Priscilla had handpainted herself. Everything about her was so . . . unusual. "I'd love to wear something like that," Gina lamented, reaching out with her fingers to gently trace a lavender iris. She glanced down unhappily at her own lemon-yellow tailored shirt and narrow, classic jeans. They definitely showed off her slim, lanky figure. In fact, it wasn't too long ago that she used to feel just right in these clothes. But, somehow, not lately . . .

"Thanks," Priscilla answered with a warm smile. "But this" — she gestured from the vest down to her baggy, faded jeans cuffed with red velvet — "is not really your look."

Gina nodded. "True," she agreed.

For the umpteenth time, Gina tried to imagine what everyone would say if she changed her look. Got crazy. Got wild. She had so much more inside than she ever let on.

If she could only just do it.

"Are you there?" Priscilla reached for Gina's shoulder and shook it gently. "Thinking about Barry Drake?"

Gina smiled. Actually, no. She wasn't. Sure, it was nice that Alexa's ex was interested. But it wasn't mutual. Mr. Athletic, straight as an arrow, handsome, A-student bored her to death.

She couldn't explain it, so she didn't let on.

Besides, it wasn't what everyone wanted to hear.

"Hello, everyone!" Vivienne called out seconds later as she and Michelle bolted into the coffee shop. Shaking her long, wavy blonde hair out of her eyes, she wrapped her deep green sweater self-consciously around her still boyish figure. "Wooo. It's frigid out there."

"You could try and be more on time," Priscilla commented dryly. "Then maybe you wouldn't get so cold."

Gina glanced at Priscilla enviously. Her thoughts exactly. The difference was, she'd have never said it. Not in a million years.

"We rushed. We really did," Margo added guiltily. "But, I mean, we saw all of you out talking anyway . . ."

"You didn't see me," Gina suddenly blurted out. Red-faced, she looked down at the table. Where had that come from?

4

It was so unlike her.

It was so risky.

For a moment, no one said a word.

Finally, Michelle cleared her voice. "We're sorry. Really."

Gina smiled with relief. "That's okay." She looked around the table. Everyone looked a little uncomfortable.

Or was it annoyed?

"I'm sorry the meeting couldn't have been at my house," Gina plunged in quickly. Nervously. "But you know my parents. They think I need to be working every minute. They'd never go for this."

Michelle nodded sympathetically. "They give you a tough time, Gina." She tucked her dark brown, shoulder-length hair behind her ears. "I'd hate it."

"You would," Gina sighed. She paused to smile at Michelle appreciatively. "But they grew up in Switzerland. It's different. They had strict parents, too."

"So, are we having a meeting?" Margo asked, looking around the table. She patted her stomach cheerfully. "I've got to do something to keep my mind off eating."

"You bet," Gina nodded. She pulled a notebook marked "The Practically Popular Crowd" from her royal-blue sports bag and flipped to the front page. Noting down the date, Gina looked around the table. "So . . ."

In spite of everything, a soft smile crept across her face.

She loved this moment. It was warm. Private. And so important. Everyone was there to support each other. To understand each other. Everyone was there to listen and bring out the best in each other. That was why they'd formed the group. And that was why she needed it so.

Gina glanced down at the notebook.

So how come she was feeling so lonely?

And, sometimes, even angry?

Lately, all she'd wanted to do was stand up and yell, "Hey! Look at me! I'm not the Gina Dumont you think I am! I'm not so agreeable. Or generous. Or good. I don't want to be so straight and hard-working!"

But she never did. It was just too scary.

What if everyone took another look at her and said, "Oh. Well, okay. But, see, Priscilla's the funky one. And we never know what to expect from Michelle. She's so emotional. And Margo's a nut. And Vivienne's a genius. Just listen to her vocabulary! And, you, well, you're the jock. The straight one. The reliable one. That's the type we need here. So, if you can't do it, good-bye."

No. She couldn't risk it.

Gina took a deep breath. "I now declare this

6

meeting of The Practically Popular Crowd in session. Who wants to begin?"

Priscilla spoke up immediately. "I'm having trouble with Mrs. Simon and algebra. I'm going to fail if I don't get some extra help. Can anyone schedule a weekly thing with me so I can keep up?" She sighed. "Boy, I wish Ms. Korf were still teaching algebra. She was so much easier! I hate it when there's a schedule change like that."

"I could try to help," Vivienne began slowly. "I've never seen you this uptight about schoolwork! I don't know about a regular schedule, but I could help tomorrow during lunch."

"How about you, Gina?" Priscilla asked. "You have everything scheduled so exactly. You must know when you have time."

"Well . . ." Gina fished her schedule card out of her bag. It was filled, except for fifteen minutes here and fifteen minutes there. She couldn't imagine how she was going to find time to flip through a magazine, or do her hair, or . . . anything. "I'm not sure, Priscilla," she replied carefully. "I'd love to help, but regularly, I don't know." She checked her schedule. "Maybe on Saturday morning I could. . . ."

"That won't work," Priscilla shook her head. "That's my art class." She set her lips together grimly. "Oh, wow. I'm in trouble. I hate asking my parents for a tutor. They'd just get at me about

7

spending too much time on my art. Oh, brother."

"Don't mention brothers," Margo interrupted. "Lewis and his part-time job are driving me nuts. All the household chores are falling to me. I stained my shirt the other day polishing the dining room table. Which reminds me, Gina, can I keep that sweater you loaned me for over the weekend? The one with the pearl buttons? I want to wear it to James's party."

"Ummmm." Gina eyed her thoughtfully. The truth was, she'd intended to wear it herself. Of course she did have others. "I sort of was planning to wear it, too. . . ."

Margo sighed. "Oh. Sure. Look, it's yours." She turned and smiled at Michelle. "How about you? Feeling generous today? I've got to wear something new. I feel like a blimp in my stuff!"

Gina nervously began doodling in her notebook. Now she'd done it.

Margo thought she was selfish. And maybe she was. How could she expect to have good friends if she couldn't be generous with her things . . . and her time?

"Look, Margo, wear the sweater," she suddenly blurted out. "Really. I'll wear the black one I have."

"Are you sure?" Margo sang out happily. "Thanks so much! I knew I could count on you! Always!"

"What about math?" Priscilla interrupted. "Can't someone give me a hand?"

"I'll work you in," Gina said quickly. "I can do it for half an hour late Friday afternoon, right before dinner." It was unlike Priscilla to be so anxious. She was usually so mature and under control. Yes — Priscilla needed help.

"You are the best," Priscilla declared, reaching across the table and squeezing Gina's hand. "You won't regret it. You are the perfect friend!"

Gina smiled. Yes. She could do everything. Give everything. Be everything to everybody. Actually, all it took was a little discipline. She had plenty of that. Ever since she was a little girl, her parents had drummed it into her. "Nothing comes easily. One must work for things. Discipline yourself. It's not always fun, but in the end . . ."

Gina the perfect.

Look how much it got her, too. Gina glanced around the table at her friends and smiled. So much love. So much approval. So much appreciation.

Suddenly, feeling the tears begin to form, she looked down at her notebook.

So much pressure.

Moving her pencil across the page, she scrawled:

TODAY WE DECIDED GINA WILL BE EVERYTHING TO EVERYBODY . . .

Gina looked up at everyone's smiling face, and then back down at the page.

. . . UNTIL SHE JUST CAN'T STAND IT ONE MORE MINUTE.

2

"I can't decide if I'm in a peach or a pink mood," Alexa Craft mused as she glanced from blush to blush. She sighed. "I actually look pretty good in both, don't you think?"

She leaned into the mirror of her white-lace-skirted dressing table and turned her head from right to left. Her thick blonde hair fell neatly into place. Alexa smiled with satisfaction.

"You do," Robin nodded, running her hands through her own short dark curls.

Alexa smiled. Robin always agreed with everything. It was really very nice. Except when it was sickening.

"I like you best in pinks," Mona replied, "but if you're in the mood for peach . . ."

Alexa nodded. Mona, on the other hand, spoke her mind.

Which was also very nice, except when it wasn't.

Alexa cocked her head to one side as she tried

11

on first a gold and then a silver dangle earring. Friends. They were such an important thing to have. Especially when they were as loyal as Mona and Robin.

Too bad she had to hide so much from them.

"So how are things with David?" Robin asked earnestly.

Alexa cringed. How had this happened? She and David were a thing already? They'd only just started spending time together.

"Why are you singling out David?" she practically hissed. "Why not Rick? Or James?"

"Oh . . . well . . ." Robin began nervously. "We . . ." — she looked at Mona beseechingly — "I thought you really liked him."

Alexa shrugged. "I do like him." She studied her reflection in the mirror. How could she tell them? It was so unbelievably obnoxious. Even for her. No. Actually, it was worse. It was . . . vapid.

Empty.

Spineless.

The truth was, she was afraid to admit how much she liked David. What if it got around?

He just wasn't popular enough. Handsome enough.

In demand enough.

It could ruin her.

Mona shrugged as she carefully braided her thick, very dark brown hair. "You always seem to have such a good time together." She paused.

"Unlike some of your past boyfriends. Barry, for instance."

Alexa looked down at the lavender straw makeup basket resting on her dressing table. This would never do.

Mona could be such a drag. Especially when she was right.

"I've had lots of fun with all my past boyfriends," Alexa lied, squaring her shoulders and looking defiantly into the mirror at Mona. She hesitated for a moment. It was simply amazing that Mona had no idea how beautiful she was. Or how popular she could be. "Forgive me, Mona, but you weren't exactly around for some of the more, shall we say, romantic moments."

Mona smiled softly. "That's true, Alexa, I wasn't."

"No, you weren't," Robin agreed. She turned to Alexa. "You drive all the guys crazy. It's obvious. Barry's just out to lunch."

Alexa nodded. As if that settled that.

Which it most certainly didn't.

The truth was, Barry dumping her was only part of the problem. She could almost manage that. It was *who* he was going after now.

Gina Dumont.

Her old friend. One of those Practically Together People or something.

It was just too much to take. Gina was thin. And athletic. And pretty. Just like Alexa.

13

In fact, it was hard to imagine why he had even bothered switching. Unless . . .

Alexa cringed at her next thought.

Unless, maybe, Gina was better.

What a nightmare.

To be tossed out for a goody two shoes. In front of everyone.

There was no question about it. Gina and Barry had to be kept apart. Somehow.

Alexa was about to lean back in her chair to consider a plan when the phone rang. She let it ring twice so that she wouldn't seem desperate. Then she picked it up.

"Alexa?"

Alexa glanced meekly at her two friends. "Hi, David." She couldn't help herself. She smiled.

"What are you up to?"

"Nothing," Alexa replied, reaching for her pink lip gloss. She waved it in the air so that Mona could see. Anything to keep her mind off the call.

Also to show her respect for Mona's opinions.

Small ways were easiest.

"Can't be," David chuckled. "You're always up to something, Alexa. You can't fool me."

"Very funny," Alexa giggled. "Actually, Robin and Mona are here."

"Oh, well, don't let me keep you," David went on quickly. "Can you grab a quick soda with me after school on Thursday?"

"You bet." Alexa smiled.

A vision of David flashed across her mind. He was definitely great. And he really seemed to get her, too.

What a drag.

If only everyone else wanted him.

"See you," he said cheerfully.

"Bye," Alexa whispered softly.

"Nice guy, that David," Mona grinned at her knowingly.

Alexa smiled weakly.

Okay, so she couldn't hide how she felt completely.

Maybe she didn't want to. Maybe she was braver and stronger than she'd thought.

A real independent thinker.

Alexa proudly lifted her chin and straightened her back.

A long, quiet moment passed, and then her shoulders began to sag.

It was such a brave thought.

It just got trapped in a very scared person.

3

Gina checked her watch. She'd finished in plenty of time. Just to be sure, she double-checked the geography quiz on her desk. It looked fine. She hadn't mixed up Norway and Sweden. And she was positive that Rome, not Naples, was Italy's capital. Satisfied, she looked around the room.

Vivienne was finished also. They caught each other's eye and smiled. Gina glanced down at the quiz once more. Uh-oh. Was Bulgaria correct? Quickly she erased the name. She switched it with Romania. There, that was better. She looked up at the ceiling. Then back at the paper. Actually, it wasn't better. She'd had it right the first time. Once more she erased the names and relabeled.

Nervously, Gina began picking at her split ends. There was no excuse for a mistake. She'd been working hard. Keeping up. Everyone knew a pop quiz was coming. There was just no reason for her to get anything less than one hundred percent.

That's what she expected. That's what her parents expected.

And that was that.

Suddenly, overwhelmingly, Gina felt like taking a long nap.

Being perfect was utterly exhausting.

If only it were easier.

If only it weren't so lonely.

If only she just didn't care anymore.

"Can I help you?" a salesperson asked at Superior Sporting Goods late Tuesday afternoon.

Gina looked up, startled. "No. No. But thanks." She turned back to the rows and rows of tennis ball cans, trying to decide how many to purchase. There was no way she could ask her parents for extra money. They'd tell her she hadn't budgeted well. That she was too wasteful. She checked her wallet. She still needed money for two lunches, a new lip gloss, and a little left over for unexpected extras. Gina frowned. That meant she could buy only one can.

How could she have been so careless?

She needed three.

Three, and to not feel so awful about it.

"Hi," an unfamiliar voice floated toward her. "You're Gina Dumont?"

Gina looked up to find a tall, rugged-looking, older boy smiling down at her. Dressed in blue jeans, a purple plaid flannel shirt, and a down vest,

17

his long, thick, wild hair reached down toward his shoulders. The effect was wildly dramatic.

Gina felt herself beginning to blush. He looked vaguely familiar. Also, exciting. But she didn't remember his name.

"Ummm . . . I'm sorry," she began. His shoulders were very broad. His eyes extremely dark green. Gina looked down self-consciously at her simple, light pink cotton turtleneck. She was getting a good figure. But it hadn't quite arrived yet.

He kept smiling. "I saw you playing tennis the other day. You looked good out there." He paused, allowing his eyes to travel over her body. "Nice legs."

Gina abruptly turned from him. Sure, her height made her look older, but she was only thirteen. He was out of line. Too personal. She picked up a can of tennis balls. So why was her heart beating so quickly?

She stole a sideways glance at him. He was still standing there, smiling at her. She took a deep breath, turned, and stared at him directly. "Do I know you?" Her voice shook ever so slightly.

"Lucas Baker," he replied. He bowed slightly.

Gina took a small step backwards. Yes. Of course. Lucas Baker. The guy with one of the fastest reputations in Port Andrews' tenth grade. What was it she'd heard about him? Crazy parties. Aggressive with girls. Very sophisticated.

Definitely not her type.

"You look worried," he continued. "I don't bite."

Gina looked down at her shoes. "I know that."

"Anyway" — Lucas took a step toward her — "I came over because I've been wanting to meet you, and a couple of people I know are getting together this weekend at the Ice Palace and I thought maybe you'd want to come."

"Oh, I . . . I . . . don't know. . . ." Gina sputtered, hating the way she sounded. Lucas Baker was asking her out? Ms. Straight? Ms. Do Everything Exactly Right? Was he nuts? Why would he be interested in her? She was too young. She didn't get around.

He did everything she wouldn't do.

He had a reputation for not caring what anyone thought.

He liked his friends to be as loose as he was.

Gina began to back up. He was wrong for her. Way too dangerous. Way too fast.

Surprisingly tempting.

In a horrible kind of way.

"Gina! Wow. Great to see you," a warm familiar voice suddenly called out. Gina whirled around to see Barry walking toward her.

Crisp, clean Barry. A knapsack filled with books weighing him down. Neat blue jeans. Buttoned-down white shirt. Short, thick brown hair. Square jaw. Blue eyes. Handsome.

Totally good. Like her.

19

Gina sighed. Actually, she hated him.

"Hi, Barry." Gina looked over at Lucas nervously. "Ummm, do you two know each other?"

"Sure," Barry replied seriously. He nodded at Lucas. "We play basketball together sometimes in the park."

"Yeah, hi, man," Lucas grinned, leaning back casually against a shelf. "How ya doin'?"

"Fine," Barry answered, clearly beginning to feel uncomfortable. "Uh, Gina, are you leaving now? Maybe I'll walk you home."

"Well, actually, I'm not," Gina suddenly blurted out. She checked her watch. What was she talking about? Of course she was going straight home. It was late. "I have a little more shopping to do here," she added. For no apparent reason.

"Oh," Barry answered, cocking his head to one side. "Okay, fine. Well, I'll see you tomorrow then." He glanced at Lucas. "Maybe I'll wander down at lunchtime . . . or at the track after school. Are you running?"

Gina nodded.

"Okay, then," Barry concluded and, with a quick awkward nod at Lucas, he turned and walked away.

"You handled that very well," Lucas grinned. "Very smooth."

"Handled what?" Gina shot back, suddenly feeling terribly uncomfortable. And embarrassed.

Why had she done that? What had gotten into her? Why was she still standing there?

"Whatever," Lucas said with a brief, deep chuckle. "Anyway, you can let me know tomorrow about Saturday if you want. I might do a little running myself." He chuckled again. "Guess there's going to be quite a crowd."

Gina nodded. For the briefest moment, Lucas leaned forward, as if he were going to kiss her. Gina stood perfectly still, petrified. But as soon as it seemed as if the kiss were inevitable, he backed off and, with a wink, ambled off.

Numb, Gina turned back to the tennis balls.

One can or three?

Barry or Lucas?

Safety or danger?

Picking up one can, Gina turned toward the register.

She took a few steps, and then doubled back for another.

Two cans. That was a good compromise.

If only the rest of her life were as easy.

The moment Gina walked through her front door, the phone began to ring.

"That's the family line, *mon cher*," Mrs. Dumont called out from her office. "It's probably for you. Pick it up in the hall, please?" She waved from her seat at the computer table.

Obediently, Gina darted into the kitchen, collapsed in a chair, and picked up the receiver. "Hello?" she said without much energy.

"Gina, you sound like you're half asleep!" Priscilla proclaimed merrily. "Are you okay?"

"Yes. Sure," Gina sighed. "I'm just tired."

"You work too hard. You do too much," Priscilla replied sympathetically. "I don't know how you do it."

So then why am I tutoring you? Gina thought to herself bitterly.

"I manage," she said quietly.

"Well, I'm just checking in," Priscilla continued. "I'm going in real early tomorrow to finish my painting. But I'll see you for lunch, okay?"

Gina hesitated. "Actually, I ran into Barry, and he said something about meeting me for lunch. . . ."

"He did!" Priscilla practically squealed. "I knew it! What did I tell you? How exciting! I'm so jealous! I promise we'll all keep away. Give you your privacy and everything."

Gina sighed. "He may not come. He was real casual about it."

"Don't be ridiculous. He'll be there. You two are perfect for each other. Trust me."

Gina considered those words for a long moment in silence.

"Priscilla," she finally murmured, "what makes you say that?"

"Say what?"

"That Barry and I are perfect for each other?"

"That's easy," Priscilla answered. "You're both smart, you're both very motivated, you're both good-looking in the same straight and perfect way, and you even dress alike! That's how come."

"I was just wondering," Gina replied slowly.

This time, Priscilla was silent for a long moment. "Is there someone else you like, Gina?"

"No," Gina answered quickly. "Not at all." Certainly not Lucas, anyway. Absentmindedly, she began drawing a pattern in the light dust that now covered the hall table.

After all, he was bad news.

If she even mentioned his name, her friends would think she was nuts.

Once again, a pair of broad shoulders clad in a purple plaid flannel shirt came into view. Along with deep dark eyes. And wild, thick long hair.

Gina looked down at her legs.

No one had ever mentioned them before.

4

Alexa stood in her bra and underpants in front of the locker room mirror. The room was bustling with activity. There were only a few minutes to spare before the bell would go off signaling gym class.

Alexa turned slightly to the right, and then the left. She smiled. Her waist could have been a pinch smaller, but really it didn't much matter. Nobody's chest was as big as hers. . . . A fact that had its pluses and minuses.

Alexa glanced over her shoulder, pretending to check the time on the wall clock. Right now it was a plus. A few girls had been watching her.

Enviously, she was quite sure.

"Alexa," Julie called out from the left. "How's David?"

"Fine," Alexa called back. She scanned the room. Was it her imagination? No one seemed that impressed. Or interested. "But you know me . . ."

she suddenly added. It was Barry's fault. He'd ruined her rep. She was slipping.

"What do you mean?" Julie asked, pulling on her shorts.

Alexa shrugged. "Well, David isn't my entire life, you know." She glanced casually around the room. But he was so funny. So warm. So reliable. In a way, for now, she really wasn't interested in anyone else. "In fact, I'm not taking him to James Wood's party on Saturday," she added.

She wasn't? Alexa could hardly believe it herself. It would have been so much fun.

Julie grinned. "I get it! You're on to someone else already!"

"Who?!" Stephanie asked quietly from behind Alexa.

Alexa whirled around to study the slim, blonde girl standing behind her. Stephanie was very cute herself. Quite popular, really. For a moment, Alexa considered asking her what she thought of David. Would she go out with him if he asked? Or would she consider herself too pretty. Or cool . . .

"Actually . . . I'm not ready to say yet," Alexa answered slowly.

Why was she being like this? It was pathetic.

What difference did it make what Stephanie thought of David? Who cared? What mattered was what *she* thought.

Not if someone else wanted him, too.

Alexa picked up her T-shirt and pulled it on.

Just because every girl in town wasn't crazy about him didn't have to mean she'd taken a step down.

Where was her confidence?

She had some. Somewhere. She was sure of it.

Only thing was, she had to find it. And fast.

Because if she didn't stop feeling like this, David was history. Like him or not.

Alexa reached for her shorts.

The sound of the bell ripped through the locker room.

She had an image to uphold.

And she had no intention of letting it slip away.

Alexa let the back door shut loudly as she stomped into the kitchen. Her knapsack dropped to the floor with an angry thump.

"Hi, Lexa, baby." Mimi, the Crafts' Jamaican housekeeper, smiled at Alexa cheerfully as she studied the local newspaper. Her pencil was moving quickly over the crossword puzzle.

"You're in a good mood," Alexa grumbled. She pulled open the refrigerator door and selected a carrot.

"I sure am," Mimi practically sang out in return. She put down her pencil. "Which makes 'bout one of us."

"What's up?" Alexa asked. "Did you win the lottery?"

"My sister just flew out for a visit. Can't wait till Friday to set my eyes on her!" Mimi smiled broadly.

Alexa nodded and forced a grin. Ah, yes. She'd forgotten. Mimi had a family. Her own family. How nice for her.

How, kind of, well, annoying.

Alexa sighed. If only her parents were around more. If only they both didn't have such impossibly busy careers, it wouldn't matter so much. But it did, and now Mimi meant everything.

It was almost embarrassing.

Alexa studied Mimi. It was her turn to say something. But what?

"You . . . you must be very excited," Alexa managed to sputter. "How long has it been since you've seen your sister?" And, when, she thought to herself, is she going home?

"A year exactly," Mimi answered promptly, as if she'd been counting the days. She began folding up the newspaper. "So, you look like you're about to blast off. What's got you all boiled up?"

Alexa shrugged. "No point discussing it." She glanced up at the cookbook shelf. "I volunteered to bake some cookies for the charity bake sale. What do you think . . ."

"You . . . you . . . did what?" Mimi laughed, an amused smile playing across her lips.

"You heard me!" Alexa replied indignantly, placing both hands on her hips. "What's the mat-

27

ter? I can't reach out and help people? What am I, the Wicked Witch of the West?"

"No, no," Mimi replied solemnly. "I don't think you're a witch. No, sir. I think you reach out a lot. It's the helpin' part that sometimes gets a little messed up, if you know what I mean." She cupped Alexa's chin in her hand. "What's goin' on?"

Alexa averted her eyes.

"Has it got somethin' to do with that nice boy who was over here the other day, stuffin' his face with my brownies?"

Alexa couldn't help herself. She chuckled. "Kind of." She stared up into Mimi's deep brown, sympathetic eyes.

"Mimi, I like David. I do. But, well, do you think he's cute?"

"You mean do I think he's as cute as that Barry?"

Alexa nodded. Leave it to Mimi. She caught on fast.

Mimi was quiet for a long minute. "Well, I'd say that kind of depends on how I'm doin' the lookin'."

"Huh?" Alexa asked, plucking a grape from the red ceramic bowl on the counter.

"I look with my ears," Mimi answered with a smile. "I'm smart." She paused to gaze at Alexa lovingly. "Sure, baby. First glance, Barry's a handsome boy. But that David. Now he gets better-lookin' when you spend some time with him."

Alexa nodded and sighed. "Yeah. I know that. You know that. Too bad other people don't think that."

Mimi shrugged. "You tryin' to tell me you're upset 'cause your friends don't think he's as cute as Barry?"

Alexa nodded. "A little. I guess." She popped another grape into her mouth. "So what's the big deal?"

"That's the saddest thing I ever heard come out of your mouth, Alexa." Mimi shook her head. "Sad and dumb."

"Well, maybe I wouldn't worry so much about my friends if Barry hadn't dumped me!" Alexa suddenly blurted out. "And now he's going after Gina Dumont. Can you believe it?"

"Some friends, if you got to worry 'bout what they think of you likin' David," Mimi harumphed. "And, Lexa baby, of course I can see him lookin' at Gina." She laughed. "Lighten up, girl! What should he do? Crawl in a hole? Go after some miserable-lookin', bad-tempered thing?"

"No," Alexa declared. "But Gina is just not acceptable."

Mimi shook her head and stood up. She moved across the room to the cookbooks. "I'd say you should spend your time lookin' for recipes and keepin' your nose out of Barry's business. In fact," she paused, leveling a steady gaze at Alexa, "I'd also spend some time bein' nice to that David. He's worth somethin', let me tell you. I know."

"Gina and Barry cannot get involved," Alexa insisted quietly, not moving from her spot. "Let him choose someone else."

"Well, there isn't much you can do 'bout it, Lexa," Mimi shrugged as she pulled a book from the shelf. "You can't control how people feel. Or what they do." She held out the cookbook. "And mark my words. If you try, you might end up all alone."

Alexa reached for the book and flashed Mimi a cocky smile.

Maybe that was true of some people. But not her. She was just too smart.

Of course, Mimi was right about one thing. She probably should just focus on David.

Alexa flipped to the index. Chocolate Puffs. Perfect.

If only David were perfect.

If only they were the only two people in the whole world.

If only she didn't have the confidence of a gnat.

5

Leaning against a tree with both hands, Gina began stretching out her calf muscles. Smoky swirls floated through the air as she practiced breathing evenly and slowly.

For the end of October, it was an unusually cold day. Gina looked over the track. Just a few people were out today. No one she knew. No Lucas.

No surprise. Who did she think she was, anyway? Scarlett O'Hara? Barry hadn't even appeared at lunch.

Gina stretched her hands to the ground.

Well, maybe after she ran, she'd feel better.

Pulling herself up to a standing position, Gina was about to do some side stretches when she felt a hand lightly tap her shoulder.

"It's *so* cold." Margo started giggling at the surprised look on Gina's face. "We couldn't let you run alone!" She began jogging in place, with a thick, bright red muffler wrapped around her neck and matching mittens. "I could use the workout, myself. You know. To drop a few pounds." She grimaced. "At least that's what Lewis said this morning."

Gina smiled sympathetically. "Your big brother's a pain."

"I'd run, too," Vivienne snickered, pulling a stopwatch out of her pocket. "But, voila! I'm afraid I have to be the official timekeeper." She planted a serious expression on her face. "That's a very critical job, you know. In fact" — she paused with a brief smile — "I think someone ought to thank me profusely for taking it on."

Gina giggled. "I will. Thanks!" Her pals. The Practically Popular Crowd. Sometimes they were the absolute greatest.

"Gina, I'd run with you. I really would," Priscilla sighed, wrapping herself up tightly in a brightly colored wool sweater coat with a fake fur collar she'd found in a thrift shop. "I'm just as slow as molasses."

"I'm not," a low, teasing voice ran out.

All four girls turned around to find Lucas Baker, hair tied back in a ponytail at the nape of his neck, standing before them in gray sweats.

No one said a word.

"So, is anyone going to join me?" he continued, obviously enjoying their surprise.

"Well . . . I'm . . . I'm . . . really not much of a runner," Michelle began taking a step backwards. "I wouldn't be fun to run with . . ." She stopped. He wasn't looking at her.

Gina looked around at her friends, who were staring at her dumbfounded. She looked back at Lucas. He wasn't taking his eyes off her.

She began jogging in place. Silently.

This was crazy. Why had he come? Why was he pursuing her? It was a silly fit. A terrible fit. Couldn't he see that? Why was he bothering her? Following her?

Exciting her?

"Oh, look!" Priscilla suddenly cried out. She pointed to a figure walking toward them from a near distance. "Barry!"

"Ah, yes," Lucas smiled. "Barry."

Gina watched as Barry drew closer, his royal-blue sweats hanging neatly on his slim, strong frame.

He looked like the all-American athlete.

He looked like an absolute heartthrob.

He looked like a horrible bore.

Abruptly, she turned to Margo. "Okay, then. Let's get going. It's too cold to stand still."

As if it were an afterthought, which it most certainly was not, she turned to Lucas. "Coming?" she asked simply, with a soft smile.

Then, as if she didn't much care about his answer, she jogged off onto the track, Margo close behind.

A few seconds later, Gina was conscious of Lucas moving easily by her side. They were both pulling slightly ahead of Margo.

"I play lacrosse, you know," he offered simply. "This is good for me."

Gina nodded. "Yes. This is good for my tennis." She turned and studied Lucas for a brief moment. So, he was into sports, too. She hadn't known that. He looked so . . . as her mother would say . . . undisciplined. Her exact opposite, really. But, actually, he wasn't.

Maybe they weren't so far apart. . . .

"What kind of mile do you run?" Lucas continued.

Gina eyed him admiringly. He seemed like a strong runner.

"About nine-and-a-half minutes. Running really isn't my sport. I just do it to keep in shape."

Lucas nodded. He turned and smiled. Then he leaned in toward her and whispered. "Given any thought to the Ice Palace? Saturday afternoon? Two o'clock. What do you say?"

Gina hesitated. Actually, she'd given it a lot of thought. She'd decided she probably could, but that it might not be such a good idea. She'd decided that she probably shouldn't, but that it could turn out well.

Mostly, she'd convinced herself he'd forget all about it.

"Well?" Lucas persisted.

Gina continued running in silence. One big problem was James's party. Her parents wouldn't let her go out all afternoon and all night. If she chose Lucas, the party was out. And her friends couldn't know why. They'd never understand. They'd disapprove. They'd try to talk her out of it. They might even win.

Or, they might even drop her.

Gina turned toward Lucas. No. She couldn't start lying. Her friends meant everything. She looked into his eyes. "No" was the only possible answer.

"Okay," Gina replied softly.

It was as if someone else had answered. Someone she didn't know.

Someone nuts.

Gina looked up at the sky. It wasn't a good idea. She was making a mistake.

He was scary. Too fast. She barely knew him.

So why was she thrilled? And if she was making a mistake, how much of a mistake could it be?

Gina glanced over her shoulder to see Margo running right behind them, a disturbed look on her face.

"I'm going to blast ahead," Lucas suddenly announced. He reached out and touched her shoulder. "I'll be seein' you." Seconds later, he was out of earshot.

Gina immediately dropped back. "Hi, there." She smiled meekly at Margo.

"You like him?" Margo asked quietly.

"I hardly know him!" Gina protested.

"I know that!" Margo shot back, her voice on the rise. "What are you doing? Barry's watching you."

Gina glanced quickly over her shoulder. It was true he had just arrived at Priscilla's side and was gazing after her. Gina looked across the track at Lucas, who was running smoothly and gracefully way ahead of them.

"Don't do it," Margo warned. "It's wrong for you."

Gina could feel the anger immediately.

When would her friends stop doing that? Telling her who she was and what she needed?

Gina clenched her fists. And when would she ever, finally, tell them to stop?

She began to pick up speed. "I'm not doing anything. Don't worry. I have to do some interval training," she murmured softly in Margo's direction.

She had to get away. Before she said something bad. Something she couldn't take back. She was vaguely conscious of Margo slowly dropping back. And completely aware of Lucas running very fast way ahead.

She started pushing hard.

Something was happening.

She could feel her heart pumping now. Fast and strong.

Was she trying to break some kind of record?

Her chest was beginning to hurt.

No. It wasn't a record she was trying to break. It was the Gina mold.

She was trying to break free of it.

She was dying to smash it to smithereens.

Gina turned and looked at Lucas.

He wasn't looking for perfect. She was sure of it. He was looking for fun. Freedom. Maybe even a little danger.

Gina felt a slight shiver go up her spine.

Sure, he wasn't exactly her type.

Yes. He was a little scary.

Probably she should have said no.

But, really, that was the whole point.

Gina Dumont was ready to do something wild.

6

"So, what little schemes have you been cooking up?" David said affectionately as he slipped an arm around Alexa's shoulders Thursday afternoon.

"How could you say that?" she answered with mock indignation. She giggled as if she were still in third grade. It felt good. Usually, with other guys, she laughed low and softly. It was, she was quite sure, much more alluring.

But all that seemed unnecessary now.

She felt very pretty just giggling.

Alexa briefly leaned her head on his shoulder. "Where are we going? The Stop? Leo's? Maybe you want to play tennis? I bet I could beat you today. I feel strong." Alexa flexed her right arm.

"Actually" — David took a long deep breath — "it's such a really neat fall day, why don't we just walk? Maybe along the aqueduct."

Alexa smiled. The aqueduct. Where people liked to bike, jog, race . . . and kiss. She looked at David out of the corner of her eye, half expecting to see him eyeing her body. Like everyone did. Especially when they talked about the aqueduct.

But he wasn't. He was just smiling. Looking around. Looking sweet.

"Sounds nice," Alexa replied softly. What an amazing feeling. It wasn't her body. It was her.

David stopped, turned, and lightly rested his lips, for just a few seconds, on hers. Nothing more. Then he turned, and once more began walking.

Alexa moved with him but, for a moment, closed her eyes. David's kisses were so warm. So meaningful. She stole a glance at him. She wanted more.

Despite his looks. Which, actually, weren't half bad.

He just wasn't fantastic-looking. And, for that, the aqueduct was good, too. It was pretty quiet. Not a lot of people to stare. Gossip. Put her down.

Though, truthfully, she wasn't sure they would. People liked him. He was cool. Relaxed. Fun. He just wasn't a "catch." He wasn't a star athlete, or full of star power.

They walked in pleasant silence for a little while.

Suddenly Alexa stopped, bent down, and picked up a tiny blue flower. "I wonder what this is called . . ." she murmured softly. "It's so pretty.

So delicate." She paused. "I wish I could frame it."

David smiled. "My mom presses flowers. It's kind of a hobby of hers. Why don't you give it a try?"

Alexa nodded enthusiastically. "Grace Kelly did that! You know. That beautiful actress who married the Prince of Monaco." Alexa lifted her own chin regally. Some people thought they looked alike.

"There you go," David chuckled. "Who knows what prince is lurking in these woods!" He gestured all around and then reached into his bag. He pulled out a book. "Here! Start pressing!"

Alexa frowned and looked away. David was teasing her. So what if she thought Grace Kelly's story was super romantic.

"Hey . . ." David tapped her on the shoulder. "Come on, Alexa. I guess I shouldn't laugh at this. My mother loves flower pressing. We've got her stuff all over the walls. Some of it's real nice." He tucked one side of Alexa's hair behind her ear. "Give it a try. I bet you'd be great, Grace."

Alexa grinned. "Really? Maybe I will. I've thought about it before. But I just never really knew where to begin."

"No excuse," David stated firmly. "Find out."

Alexa smiled softly. She would. Absolutely.

"Oh, look," David interrupted her thoughts. "There's Stephanie and Pete Ward."

"Oh, yes," Alexa said, oozing an "Oh, isn't that nice" attitude she distinctly didn't feel.

Pete was quite handsome. She never liked him much. He had a kind of stupid sense of humor. But girls liked him.

And that was nothing to sneeze at.

She glanced at David's face. He had kind of a biggish nose. But very nice blue eyes. And a terrific smile. His face was a little too round. Her eyes traveled down to his high-top white sneakers. He did have a nice slim body. A little skinny, maybe.

Alexa frowned.

She moved ever so slightly away from David. Instantly, he dropped his arm from around her shoulder. He glanced at her questioningly, but Alexa pretended not to see.

"Hi, Stephanie," she said gaily. "Peter."

"Hello, you two." Stephanie smiled. "What's up?"

Alexa tried to fight her annoyance. "You two" was not the way she wanted to be known. It was okay that people knew she was seeing David. That was fine. But "you two" sounded too exclusive. Too tied up.

Or, rather, tied down.

"We're admiring the flowers," David joked. He smiled at Alexa. "And a few other things."

"We're just walking," Alexa shrugged quickly. "Talking." Why was she feeling so embarrassed?

41

"Right . . . us, too . . ." Stephanie giggled, giving Pete a flirtatious look. Alexa watched as Stephanie gave David a good looking over. A moment later Stephanie smiled at her, and then up at Pete.

Alexa wanted to smack her. She was showing off. She was saying, "Mine is better." She was saying, "Compare the two and you decide."

Alexa looked away.

Why did she feel so awful? So mixed up? So torn?

Why hadn't she dumped Barry before he dumped her? After all, it wasn't like she'd ever really cared about him.

"Well, we'd better get going," Pete grinned at David. "See you tomorrow. Have a good time." Nodding at Alexa, Pete turned and started walking, his arm wrapped possessively around Stephanie's shoulder.

Alexa sighed as they ambled off. She turned to David and smiled tentatively.

She was very confused.

"So," David remarked, slipping his arm through hers. "What's with you? You don't want anyone to know we're seeing each other?"

For a long moment, Alexa froze.

People usually didn't do this. They didn't call her on things. They didn't catch on so fast. They let her do what she wanted.

"Hey, Alexa, relax!" David laughed, shaking

her arm slightly. "I was just kidding. You just seemed so nervous in front of them. What's with you?"

"Nothing . . ." Alexa blurted out. "Really." She took a deep breath. That was close. Way too close.

Still, the undeniable truth was finally before her.

She wanted David, and she wanted her popularity, too. And if she couldn't have them both up front, then one of them would have to move to the side.

And that one would probably be David.

Alexa smiled meekly in his direction.

"Oh. You're making nice again?" he asked, smiling back.

"Sure am," Alexa nodded, looking away shyly. Guiltily.

One problem, though. He'd have to cooperate.

He'd have to play the game.

David wasn't good at that.

That's why she liked him.

And that was why she'd have to work very hard to keep him . . . in the dark.

7

Gina sat on the floor of Priscilla's room, picking on the long threads of the lime-green rug and feeling as if she were going to burst. Right there. Just fly into one thousand pieces.

Priscilla was talking. It was her emergency meeting. Something about flunking a math quiz. Something about not feeling smart. Gina pulled a piece of lime-green yarn free and began twirling it between her thumb and forefinger.

She looked around the room. Her friends. Her crowd.

And yet they had no idea. She looked the same. She sounded the same. She dressed the same.

But she wasn't the same.

She had a delicious, an exciting, an almost frightening secret.

And it wasn't just Lucas Baker.

It was Gina Dumont. The new Gina Dumont.

Gina the wild and crazy.

Her eyes traveled around the circle. They

44

wouldn't approve. They wouldn't understand. They'd try to talk her out of it.

They might even win.

"Let's face it," Priscilla sighed. "I guess I'm just meant to be an artist. Good grades are a thing of the past."

"Not that again!" Vivienne cried out playfully, smacking her hand against her forehead. "That's ridiculous! You're very smart and you know it. You have a good sense of humor. You know the name of every painter and painting you see! You write fantastically. What are you talking about?!"

"So why am I suddenly not doing so well in school?" Priscilla moaned.

"Maybe because you don't do your homework," Vivienne suggested matter-of-factly.

Gina studied her friends guiltily. Sadly. Actually, she wanted to tell them. It just wouldn't work.

"You do spend a lot of time in the art studio," Michelle interjected. "Also at your art school. Honestly. That would make it hard for anyone."

Priscilla shrugged. "It can't be helped. My art means everything to me."

"That's an excuse," Margo shook her head. "You're just saying that so you don't have to try."

Priscilla smiled meekly. "Maybe."

"Anyway, Gina's helping you on Friday afternoons. And I'll help, too," Vivienne reminded her. "You'll do fine. It's important. We'll all help."

"Fine." Michelle laughed. "Now, what's everyone wearing to James's party?"

Gina could feel herself tense. The time had come.

The lying was about to begin. There was no other way.

"Wait," she suddenly blurted out, playing for time. "Maybe Priscilla isn't through." Actually, why couldn't she tell them? They weren't her parents. They were her friends. So what if they didn't approve? She didn't always like everything they did, either. They wouldn't just leave her. Of course not.

How silly.

"It's okay." Priscilla waved an arm through the air. "Really. I feel better just getting it out. I think I'm going to wear my red silk antique dress." She smiled at Gina. "What about you?"

Gina quickly looked away. The room grew oddly silent. She cleared her throat and glanced at Margo, who was staring at her intently. She'd intended to simply call late Saturday afternoon and say she was sick.

"Well," Gina began slowly, not at all sure what was going to come out: an outfit description, or Lucas's name. "I'm not sure," she finally murmured.

"Is something wrong with you?" Michelle asked curiously. "You look a little funny."

Gina shook her head slightly. "Wrong? No. Nothing is wrong."

What if she told them and they talked her out of it? Really they should. Lucas was bad news. Everyone said so.

"Gina, something's up with you," Vivienne insisted. "It's evident by the look on your face. In fact, where were you at lunch today?"

Gina bit down on her lower lip and studied Vivienne quietly. She'd been hiding. Besides, Viv was the last person to understand what was happening. She hadn't had much to do with boys yet.

Then, again, Gina wasn't at all sure she knew what was happening, either. "I . . . I . . . I'm not sure what I'm wearing. That's all." She shrugged. "I can't decide."

"By the way, what was all that about Lucas yesterday?" Priscilla asked. "I couldn't believe it! I meant to call you last night."

Gina hesitated, and then very slowly shook her head. "That was something, wasn't it," she said with disinterest. Boredom.

It was amazing. She was lying, and it was coming so easily. She was being so . . . secretive.

It was actually horribly exciting.

"What did he want?" Priscilla persisted. "I saw you guys talking."

"He just was asking me about my running time. That's all."

So many lies. Gina looked from girl to girl, smiling evenly. And why not? No one was getting hurt.

Gina began pulling once again at the threads of Priscilla's green carpet.

Maybe this was the answer. She could appear to be everything everyone wanted, but on the side . . .

The possibilities were endless. A secret boyfriend like Lucas! A secret hobby, like . . . jazz dancing! Maybe even a secret wardrobe filled with fabulous clothes. Sexy clothes. Tight clothes.

"Barry is going to be there, you know," Michelle piped up. "James told me he invited him at the last minute, along with a few of his friends."

"Oh," Gina answered quickly. She looked around the room. Everyone was smiling at her happily.

And why not?

She did everything right.

She did what everyone expected.

No surprises.

Only, now, she had a secret life.

Lucas on one side. Everyone else on the other.

Ms. Perfection here. Ms. Caution-to-the-Wind there.

Satisfaction everywhere.

Gina frowned. It couldn't possibly be that easy.

8

Friday afternoon Alexa stood in the middle of her walk-in closet, considering the contents. A growing pile of clothes rested at her feet as she paired and then discarded a black sweater with green pants, a red blouse with a denim skirt, and tight blue jeans with a sequined workshirt.

Alexa stamped her foot in exasperation. Nothing looked right. Of course, maybe that was because nothing felt right. The truth was, she didn't want to spend time flirting with other guys at James's party. She just wanted to see David.

But that simply couldn't be. She had a plan.

And it was called Operation Invisible Love.

Alexa hesitated, a melancholy smile beginning to form. Actually, she and David were sort of like star-crossed lovers. The Romeo and Juliet of Port Andrews Junior High.

She could see herself now on the balcony. Beckoning . . .

The similarities seemed magnificently endless.

Romeo and Juliet were young and in love.

Alexa and David were young and heavily in like.

Romeo and Juliet had to hide from their families.

Alexa and David had to hide from her friends. . . .

Spotting an oversized black scoop-neck sweater, and black-and-fluorescent-green leggings, Alexa plucked them off their hangers and slipped them on.

Not bad. She was about to reach for a chain belt when the phone rang.

"Alexa?" David's warm voice danced across the wire.

"Hi!" Alexa responded a bit too hysterically.

What if he asked her out Saturday night? Everything depended on her getting time alone. Just Alexa and every other guy at the party.

"Well, you sound happy," David chuckled. "Is it me?"

Alexa hesitated. Actually, it was. Kind of. "I suppose so," she replied softly.

"Listen, I just wanted to tell you that I ran into James Wood, and he invited me and Barry to his party. You're going, right?"

Alexa sat down cross-legged on the floor and rolled her eyes.

Operation Invisible Love was off to a very bad start. How was she going to look like Miss Available with David hanging around? She'd never get a chance to prove in front of everyone that she could land anyone at any time.

And what about Barry and Gina making a fool of her? She still hadn't worked out a way to keep them apart. What a mess.

"Yeah, I'm going. . . ." Alexa replied, more unhappily than she had intended.

And then it hit her. It was such a simple idea. Her favorite sort, really. The kind that worked so well because it twisted things just enough for great results, but not enough to get her into trouble.

Operation Invisible Love. Phase One. Put David on a schedule.

"You know, David," Alexa began, her voice dripping with helpfulness, "I've been to James's parties before. I know he says they start at seven-thirty. But don't show up until a quarter to nine. It isn't worth it. No one comes till then."

"Oh . . ." David hesitated. "Well, okay, then. I won't." He paused again. "Thanks for telling me. I'll see you tomorrow night." And with that, he chuckled and blew a kiss over the phone.

Alexa grinned, blew one back, whispered goodbye, and hung up.

What a dirty business.

There were other guys out there. Good-looking ones. Popular ones. She didn't know anyone she particularly liked, but that didn't matter.

What mattered was she had to be seen with them.

Make her statement. Throw everyone off the track.

David didn't really have to know, either.

She could pull it off. She was positive of it.

Sure, Romeo and Juliet died at the end. But they had made a mess of things. Planned poorly. Jumped to conclusions.

Very sad, really.

But that was just a play. This was real life.

And Alexa Craft was in control.

More or less.

"It's no use," Priscilla sighed, tossing her wide-brimmed black hat onto Gina's bed. "I've probably been breathing too many paint fumes. My brain cells are dying."

"You can do it," Gina insisted quietly. She placed a blank sheet of paper on top of a magazine and handed it to Priscilla. "Now, let's go."

She said it almost sharply. Instantly, Priscilla looked up at her with surprise.

"Sorry," Gina said, grabbing Priscilla's hand and squeezing it. "I'm just tired."

Funny, Lucas or no Lucas, actually she was annoyed. She didn't want to be doing this. She had her own work.

She had her own plans.

But she couldn't let on. Not if she wanted friends.

Gina smiled nicely at Priscilla. Harmless lies. That's all these were. A small price to pay for a whole new life.

She coughed once, waited a few seconds, and coughed again. "I'm not feeling too well, actually."

"Oh, no!" Priscilla exclaimed. "What about James's party?"

Gina shrugged. "I'm going to try to be there." She sighed. "I hope I make it."

For the briefest moment, Gina felt terrible. Beginning a secret life was a complicated thing. A deceitful thing.

Lucas's deep brown eyes flashed before her.

A wild, unpredictable thing.

"Now" — Gina picked up a pencil, all business — "try this problem." She began writing:
$$2x + 3 = 5.$$

Priscilla cocked her head to one side. "Okay, well, I have to find out what x equals, so first I have to get the x by itself. Right?"

"Very good," Gina nodded. She paused. What was she going to wear tomorrow afternoon to the skating rink? Sweats or a skating skirt?

"So how do I do that?" Priscilla asked.

"Do what?" Gina replied absentmindedly. Exactly how short was that skating skirt? It was last year's. Probably very short.

"GET THE X ALONE," Priscilla answered loudly. "Gina, you're not concentrating!"

"Sorry," Gina mumbled. Quickly, she picked up her pencil and scribbled $2x = 2$ on the sheet of paper in front of Priscilla. She might be asking for trouble if she wore it.

"That's nice," Priscilla commented, her voice dripping with sarcasm. "I'm so glad you know what you're doing. Really. It's thrilling."

Gina nodded, suddenly stood up, and threw open the bottom drawer of her bureau. The skirt had to be there. In fact, her skating tights were probably stuck at the bottom right along with it. Moving aside two heavy, bright-colored cable-knit sweaters, she spotted the red nylon skirt crushed under an assortment of gloves and scarves. She was about to yank it out when something stopped her.

She turned to glance at Priscilla. She had the strangest feeling Priscilla was upset.

"Ummmm." Gina pushed the drawer shut and leaned toward the paper. "How are you doing?"

"How am I doing?" Priscilla asked. "Not well. It might have something to do with the fact that you aren't explaining anything to me, but I'm not sure."

"I . . . I'm sorry," Gina stammered. She smiled sheepishly at her friend. "What don't you understand?"

"I don't understand how you got $2x = 2$."

"I subtracted 3 from each side. Remember, whatever you do to the left you have to do to the right."

Priscilla nodded. "Okay. I guess."

Gina looked down at her hands. Actually, it wasn't okay.

She wasn't being very helpful at all.

But, then, she'd never really wanted to be in the first place.

She studied Priscilla's unhappy expression.

Gina the perfect was slipping already.

It was a little frightening.

Quickly, she pulled out some fresh paper.

"Let's do it again." She smiled at Priscilla encouragingly. "You'll get it. I promise. You'll understand everything soon."

She started writing.

This double life thing was tricky.

A little time with her. A little time with him.

Concentrate here. Concentrate there.

Keep it separate. Don't confuse the two.

Gina sighed. Okay, so it wouldn't be easy.

$x = 1$. Just as long as it worked.

9

Gina stood in the locker room of the Ice Palace and shivered ever so slightly. She wasn't cold. Her heavy blue-and-red wool sweater was cozy. And though her skating skirt was rather short, her bright red tights were snug and warm.

Gina wrapped her arms around her chest and tried to calm herself. So what if she'd come here alone? No friends. No security. She was in eighth grade. She wasn't a baby. And if Lucas proved to be too much for her . . . well, then, she'd just walk away.

If she could. He was so . . . so . . .

"Ummm . . . aren't you Gina Dumont?" a loud, cheerful voice rang out.

Gina spun around to find herself standing next to a tall, slim girl dressed in black leggings and a long black-and-purple turtleneck sweater. Her dark hair was piled loosely on top of her head, with tendrils lightly falling over her forehead and down her neck. Her eyes were heavily made up with black liner and lavender shadow. The effect was extremely exotic. Not to mention intimidating.

Gina nodded. "I am." She paused. "Have we met before?" she asked politely. The embarrassment was immediate. Her words were too formal. Too well-brought-up.

The girl laughed. Gina cringed. She sounded ridiculous. She sounded as if she were talking to her parents' friends. But that was no surprise. When Gina got tense, Gina got perfect.

"Actually, no," the girl replied finally. A friendly smile settled on her face. "I'm Lucas's good friend, Mara. I go out with his best friend, Taylor. Lucas sent me in here to look for you." She stepped back and studied Gina from head to toe. "Nice outfit."

Gina looked away quickly. It was hard to tell if Mara meant it. Next to Mara's sophisticated getup, she looked like a stupid snow bunny.

Mara placed a hand on Gina's arm. "Hey, I mean it. I don't say things I don't mean."

Gina nodded. Whatever. She still looked five years younger than Mara. "Lucas is out there, then?" Gina looked into the mirror. It was no use. Sure she looked good. But she looked like Gina Dumont. Girl drip. Not a hair out of place. A bit of blush. A touch of lip gloss. A lot of nothing.

She glanced at Mara self-consciously. "I . . . I . . . didn't have time to put on much makeup this morning," she lied. "I slept late."

Mara shrugged. "No problem. Here ya go." Reaching into her bag, she pulled out a tube of black mascara, a three-color eyeshadow kit, and some pink lip liner.

Gina accepted them gratefully and quickly applied the mascara. Snapping open the eye shadow kit, she paused. She'd never used the stuff before. "I'm not sure these are my colors," she began lamely, studying the shades of lavender and blue . . . as if she knew what she was doing . . . as if past experience proved other tones were better.

"Oh, no. They are. Let me," Mara offered quickly. "The medium blue is right for you. Here . . ." And with a confident hand, she swept some color onto Gina's lids. Then cupping Gina's chin in her hand, she applied the lip liner. "Do you have some gloss with you?" Mara asked. Gina nodded, silently handed it to her, and stood completely still as Mara finished up her work.

Mara stepped back and considered the effect. "Much better. More dramatic." She grinned at Gina. "I'd like to be a makeup artist for movies someday. Take a look at it yourself."

Gina turned to study herself in the mirror.

She caught her breath. She actually looked beautiful. Older, too. Glamorous, even.

She could get to love this secret life.

"Come on. We're all waiting for you. Lock your stuff up. It's skating time!" Mara laughed.

Shoving her bag in a locker and slipping on her own combination lock, Gina took a deep breath and followed Mara out the door. She wobbled slightly as the blades of her skates traveled along the rubber flooring.

Gina grimaced. She'd have wobbled if she were wearing sneakers. Her nerves were on fire. She felt like an imposter. An actress. A spy. Completely and utterly unlike herself.

And the question was, how bad was that?

Herself was a drag.

"You skate very well," Lucas smiled down at Gina. His arm was tucked firmly around her waist.

"Thanks," Gina smiled softly, not daring to look at him. She glanced down at their skates, gliding rhythmically, magically, perfectly together.

What was happening to her? She'd never felt this way before. She felt so deliciously . . . naughty . . . and excited. Briefly, she glanced up at Lucas. It was unbelievable. It felt like being in someone else's life.

Or in a wonderful play. Or movie. With Mara as the makeup artist! Gina began to giggle at the thought.

"What's up?" Lucas asked as he looked down at her questioningly. Suddenly he executed a quick

59

turn and, skating backwards directly in front of her, slipped both hands around her waist. "You're beautiful, Gina. . . ." he began.

Gina grinned happily.

"I'd like to get to know you better," Lucas went on. His eyes traveled from her eyes down across her body.

Gina tensed ever so slightly.

Real life was getting in the way.

Gina cleared her throat. She turned to her right desperately, looking for some diversion. Something to talk about. Something to break Lucas's obvious train of thought.

But her eyes fell upon Mara and Taylor standing in the corner of the rink, arms around each other, kissing. Deeply.

Suddenly her eyes lit on a familiar blonde head. Alexa Craft was just exiting through the large glass double doors.

Gina quickly looked back up into Lucas's eyes. She was too young for this. Too inexperienced. Alexa could handle him better.

"I don't mean to rush you, Gina," he began.

Gina nodded silently. Okay, so he knew she was nervous. That was good. She felt her body relax just a bit.

Of course, it was also bad. This was the new Gina Dumont. Not the other one. That was the whole point. She didn't want to be treated like the goody Gina.

"You're not rushing me," she smiled brightly. Falsely. "I'm fine." Gina placed her hands lightly over his, as if to say, "I'm not afraid. I am up to this."

Lucas responded by leaning forward and lightly kissing her on the lips. His mouth lingered over hers. Gina had never been kissed that way before. Once, over the summer, a guy had French-kissed her. But it was awkward. And she hadn't liked the taste.

This was different.

It was romantic. Sexy.

A little frightening.

It was a kiss that made her feel older. Mature.

Lucas pulled away and swung back along her side. Once again, his arm slipped firmly around her waist.

Gina heaved a sigh of relief. This wasn't so hard.

Gina Dumont could handle more than she'd expected.

Gina Dumont was a lot more than just a good girl.

Gina Dumont had a new and wonderful secret life.

She looked down at the rink.

If only Gina Dumont weren't skating on such thin ice.

10

"**H**ello, everyone!" Alexa called out as she confidently swung open James's front door. "Where's the host?" she added jokingly. Her eyes traveled about the room.

Spotting James standing in the corner talking with a few friends, she waved. He grinned back. Alexa nodded and smiled warmly. She couldn't help herself.

He was doing it again. That *I'd do anything for you* look. Alexa blew him a kiss, and quickly slipped out of her fake-fur-lined jean jacket. James was such a sweet boy. It was lovely to have him always there. Waiting. Hoping. Again, her eyes scanned the room.

"Hey, Alexa," Julie called out. "You look great!"

"Alexa, where are you going to be tomorrow?" someone else's voice sang out.

Alexa shrugged and nodded in both directions.

Actually, what Julie said was true. Her ice-blue

form-fitting V-necked sweater looked glorious over the almost identically colored skintight cords she was wearing. And even she had noticed her blue eyes seemed to positively shimmer as a result.

Which was a good thing.

David didn't seem to be there, and already she'd spotted two very attractive boys from the ninth grade.

One of them, in fact, was Randy Stern, an up-and-coming basketball star. Tall. Nice-looking. Not gorgeous, but very sexy. Alexa watched him for a moment. Cocky, too. He was leaning against a wall, chatting with a few very attentive girls.

He looked so smug. It was almost sickening.

Still, he was exactly the right place to start.

Phase Two. Land some guys in public.

Sucking in her stomach, Alexa began to move toward them. On the way, she picked up a handful of pretzels. She had no intention of eating them. They were a prop. A casual note to a well-planned moment.

"Hello, Nina." Alexa smiled sweetly at a cute, dark-haired girl who was now gazing admiringly up into Randy's intense green eyes.

"Oh . . . uh . . . hi," Nina answered almost unhappily.

For a brief moment, Alexa was tempted to walk away. Poor Nina. She was trying to interest Randy. And here Alexa had confused matters in no time flat. She hadn't checked yet, but Alexa was absolutely positive Randy's eyes were now glued on her.

"So, how's school treating you?" Alexa continued, staring straight at Nina. As if Nina were the most fascinating creature around. Never mind the fact that she'd barely said a word to her since school started.

"Fine . . . fine . . ." Nina replied softly.

Slowly, Alexa turned to smile at Randy who, just as she had suspected, was gazing intently, admiringly, at her.

Well, actually, her body.

Which, under the circumstances, was fine with her.

Especially given the time pressures.

"Hello, Randy," she said in a low, soft voice. "I've been hearing a lot about you and the hoop. . . ."

"Yes?" Randy asked. His body shifted ever so slightly toward her and away from Nina. "Any details?"

"Oh, just that you're very good." Alexa laughed softly and deeply. "But you know that, don't you?"

"I suppose," Randy grinned, leaning casually back against the wall, his eyes boring into hers.

Hearing some new voices at the door, Alexa turned to make sure David had not arrived.

Then she glanced back at Randy. Time was running out.

She had to make a splash.

A statement.

A kind of declaration of her popularity.

Aggressive action was in order. Right now.

Flirtatiously, Alexa slipped her arm through Randy's and gently pulled him over to the refreshment table.

There were so many people there. No one could miss them.

"I'm terribly thirsty. Let's get something to drink."

Out of the corner of her eye, Alexa saw Nina quietly slink off with the other girls who had been occupying Randy's time.

Okay. The world could see Alexa Craft was still in control.

"So," Alexa began, speaking just loud enough for those people immediately surrounding them to hear, "I didn't realize you were friends with James. I've never seen you two together."

"Yeah, well, we hang out sometimes," Randy replied. His eyes were not on her face.

Alexa could see Stephanie staring right at them. Alexa moved a step closer to Randy. "You know, my soda is flat. Can I have a sip of yours?" she asked. Without waiting for an answer, she tipped Randy's glass, which he was still holding, toward her lips.

She glanced at Stephanie and then down at the glass.

An intimate moment. Perfect. Things were going very well.

"So, Alexa, I saw you at the last basketball game. . . ."

Alexa lowered her eyes, as if she were feeling a tad bashful. "I didn't see you looking at me," she replied softly, as if she were surprised and pleased.

Suddenly, she felt his free hand slip around her waist.

"I was," he replied simply. "Trust me."

Alexa nodded. And cringed just a little. Actually, Randy was a little slimy. Phony. Not real and fun, like David.

David. Where was he? On the one hand, she couldn't wait to see him. On the other, she wasn't quite through scoring points with Randy.

She glanced quickly over Randy's shoulder. The room was definitely watching. Stephanie was huddled in a corner with Julie, talking feverishly. James kept turning around and staring at her. Margo and Michelle were standing directly to her right, and she could tell they were intently listening to every word she and Randy exchanged.

Alexa smiled and looked up at Randy. Things were going better than expected. What a perfect solution she'd come up with! A flirtation here, an attraction there, and David when everything else was in order.

There was just that small matter of keeping

Gina away from Barry to complete the almost-perfect picture. But that would come. She was sure of it. Of course, what *was* Gina doing with Lucas Baker at the rink that afternoon?

"David!" Mona's voice rang out above the crowd. "Hi!"

Alexa whirled around to see David walk through the door, followed closely behind by Barry. Quickly, she turned and shot Mona a grateful glance.

Then she ever so slightly moved a bit to the left.

Randy's hand slipped to his side.

"Oh, I see someone I have to say hello to," Alexa began. She placed her hand on his briefly. "I'll be back. . . ."

She started heading straight for David when, suddenly, she stopped. Jumping to his side would be the wrong move. It would be a "you're my boyfriend" move. It was just what she didn't want. Not there. Not out in the open. Making a sharp turn to her left, Alexa approached Mona and Robin, who were standing by the window.

"Hi, guys," Alexa smiled cheerfully.

"What's up with Randy?" Mona replied with a shake of her head.

"Nothing, really," Alexa shrugged her shoulders. She looked down at her shoes. It was a drag keeping secrets from Mona. But this was something Mona would never appreciate. She just didn't care about staying on top. Of course, most people admired Mona. She just didn't know it. Which was a good thing . . . for Alexa, anyway. It made Mona stick like glue. Who knew what she'd do if she found out? For a brief moment, Alexa felt a deep and painful pang of jealousy for her very closest friend.

"Randy is cute," Robin interrupted. She smiled at Alexa encouragingly. "We're not trying to stop you or anything."

"Well, that's good of you," Alexa snapped. Then she shrugged apologetically. What did she expect? What was Robin supposed to be — a mind reader?

"Here comes David." Mona smiled over Alexa's shoulder. Quickly she grabbed Alexa's hand. "I don't know what you're up to," Mona whispered urgently, "but I don't think David is the type to sit still while you run over him with a steam-roller."

Alexa nodded and grinned.

"Hi, kiddo," David smiled at her warmly. He threw his arm around her shoulders and kissed her lightly on the cheek. For a split second, Alexa impulsively leaned in close and gently rubbed her cheek against his wool cranberry vest. Then, quickly, she moved away.

"So, Mona, I know how Alexa is. How are you? How did the debate go?"

"Terrific," Mona replied brightly. She grinned

at Alexa. "Especially after Alexa taught me her tricks!"

"Oh," David chuckled, "and what were those?"

"How to act like you're sure of yourself when you're really not," Mona laughed.

"Hmmmmm," David answered. He turned and stood directly opposite Alexa. "I see. You're a past master at that?"

Alexa smiled. "Well, I don't always feel that way. Sometimes I feel perfectly sure of everything." She squared her shoulders almost defiantly. "I'm tough, you know."

"Yeah?" David laughed. "Prove it!"

Alexa started giggling. "I can't do that, David. Like how? Come on!"

"Sure you can!" David chuckled, patting her cheek affectionately. "Convince me that . . . that . . ."

"Don't!" Alexa laughed. "You're embarrassing me. It has to just happen. Stop!"

"Is someone bothering you, Alexa?" a low voice interrupted.

Alexa whirled around to find Randy standing close beside her, watching David curiously.

"No . . . no . . ." Alexa stammered.

"It sure sounded that way," Randy persisted with a half-smile on his face. "I wouldn't want anyone bothering you."

"It's okay, really," Alexa replied. She glanced

around to find a number of people staring right at them. This was not what she had had in mind. Not at all.

She had intended to keep things very separate. Very clean.

"Well, I think she answered your question," David interjected, smiling nicely at Randy. "She's in good hands. Okay?"

Randy shrugged. "Okay." He nodded and winked at Alexa. "I'll be waiting. . . ." he whispered loud enough for everyone to hear, and then ambled off.

"Well, I guess you were pretty busy before I got here, weren't you?" David asked, tilting his head to one side. "I mean, don't let me cramp your style, Alexa."

"You're not . . . I mean, I wasn't. . . ." Alexa stammered unhappily. Darn Randy. She leaned her head lightly on David's shoulder. "You're taking that all wrong. I don't care about Randy. I really don't."

She could feel David let out a deep breath. "Well, I'm glad to hear that," he replied, his voice warmer now. "I guess you can't help it if guys drop dead over you."

Alexa nodded. That was true.

It was also a very close call.

"Has anyone seen Gina?" a low soft voice suddenly rang out close by.

Alexa whirled around to see Barry looking at Julie.

And Julie and Stephanie staring at her.

That was it. She'd let it go too long.

Alexa smiled up at David. She was crazy about him. But this thing with Barry was driving her nuts.

It didn't make a lot of sense, but Alexa was used to that.

Popularity was a difficult business.

One had to do all kinds of crazy stuff to stay on top.

Operation Invisible Love, Phase Three:

Roses are Red,
Violets are Blue
Gina, get set
for a trick or two. . . .

11

Sunday afternoon Alexa sat in the Crafts' red plush paisley den, watching baseball with her father and flipping through magazines for history class.

Her mind was spinning. It was hard to concentrate. She picked up her scissors. What had the teacher said? Something about cutting out names from ancient Greek or Roman culture.

Still, what *was* Gina doing with Lucas Baker at the Ice Palace?

Her eyes rested on *PANTHEON THEATER*. Alexa started snipping.

She frowned. It didn't make any sense. Barry was Gina's type. She had to be crazy about him. Alexa shook her head.

How was she supposed to tear them apart if she didn't know what was going on?

Alexa flipped a few pages. *ACROPOLIS RESTAURANT*. *Authentic Greek Fare*. Again, Alexa began to cut.

Lucas and Gina. Could something actually be happening between them? Mr. Fast with Ms. Goody Two Shoes? Talk about getting in over one's head.

Alexa began to smile. Gina had to be out of her mind.

How perfect.

Alexa's eyes rested on *VENUS HAIR SALONS*. Her smile widened. Venus. Goddess of Love. Her middle name. She flipped her blonde hair back over her shoulders. Or at least it ought to be.

A vision of Barry and Gina flashed across her mind once more. It certainly wouldn't be if they got together. Especially now. So soon after his, well . . . Alexa frowned. Rejection was too harsh. Not accurate, really. It was more a certain lack of enthusiasm.

No. Gina had to be knocked out of the picture. And right now, Lucas Baker seemed the best way. Alexa looked up at the ceiling thoughtfully. Most relationships needed a little encouragement.

Alexa reached for the phone.

An excuse. She needed a good one to call. Suddenly her face lit up. The bake sale.

"YES!" Mr. Craft suddenly cried out.

Alexa looked up, startled. She hadn't been talking out loud, had she? And, anyway, it wasn't that good an idea.

"HOME RUN!" he continued, popping up from his seat with both hands in the air.

Alexa smiled tolerantly and reached for the phone.

A home run. How nice. She could use one of those, too.

Things were getting out of hand.

Gina sat at her desk, flipping through magazines.

MERCURY MESSENGER SERVICE. Gina picked up her scissors, neatly snipped out the oblong ad, and placed it on the pile that was growing very slowly to her right.

If only Lucas hadn't invited her to a party next Saturday night.

Filled with nervous energy, Gina stood up and began pacing her room, the magazine in hand. What she really needed to do was talk to her friends.

Her eyes caught the image of a trident. *NEPTUNE FISH MARKET*. Gina walked back to her desk. She began snipping. The party was too much for her. She wouldn't know anyone. His crowd was older than she. Gina wasn't used to going places without at least one of her friends. And, besides, her parents would never let her go if they knew the details. She was going to have to lie.

To everyone.

Gina put the scissors down on her desk.

A frantic feeling began to take hold. What was she doing? One date with Lucas Baker, and she was twisting her life into a pretzel.

Getting weird on her friends.

Gina closed her eyes. She should back out now. Before she lost everything. Lucas just made her feel too nervous.

Also fabulous.

Still, there had to be another way to break free. . . .

But he was so . . . cool.

Besides, how could she go back to the way things had been?

She couldn't. It was too late. She had to see this through.

It was fun getting wild. Being daring. Acting older.

Just not alone. Just not all the time.

If only she could talk to someone about it. Like Michelle. Maybe even take her to the party. She was so understanding about Gina's parents. Maybe she'd understand this, too.

But she'd tell the group, and then they'd all be on top of her. Disapproving. Maybe even getting mad. Worse, maybe even making her feel like she didn't belong anymore.

Gina could feel the tears beginning to form.

She had to go to that party. She had to see

Lucas again. Kiss him again. Hug him again. Something new was happening inside her. Something great. She could feel it.

Gina flipped a few pages of her magazine.

The ache was intense.

She needed to talk to someone. Badly.

She glanced at the phone.

But who?

A moment later, it began to ring.

"Hi, Gina," Alexa began in a pleasant enough tone. It was important not to sound too friendly right off. Gina would get suspicious. "It's Alexa."

"Oh . . . hi . . ." Gina replied uncertainly.

Alexa cleared her throat. Something told her to start talking fast. "I was just wondering what kind of cookies you're planning to bake. I don't want to double up."

"Cookies?" Gina asked. Total silence followed.

Alexa waited a few seconds. Nothing happened. Gina was a thousand miles away.

"Gina? Are you okay?" she asked. Alexa furrowed her brow. This was going nowhere fast.

"I'm sorry," Gina responded quickly. "Cookies. I don't know. I've been all caught up thinking about something else. . . ."

Alexa paused. Actually, maybe things were going better than she'd thought. Patience. That was the key.

"That's okay," Alexa answered carefully. She

had to step lightly. She could feel it. "What's up?" she said softly. Invitingly. She hoped.

"Nothing, really," Gina answered quietly.

Almost, Alexa had the feeling, reluctantly.

This was as good a time as any.

"Did I see you at the Ice Palace with Lucas Baker?"

For a moment, she thought she'd gone too far, too fast.

Gina didn't say a word for what felt like a year.

"Yes, you did," she finally answered. "It was nothing."

Alexa chuckled. "It didn't look that way to me. I was impressed."

Again, Gina didn't say a word.

"Do you like him?" Alexa asked, she hoped, sweetly. And with sincere, innocent interest.

"I . . . I — " Gina began, obviously not sure if she wanted to go on.

"Yes?" Alexa interjected gently.

" — don't know," Gina finally finished. "I really don't."

Alexa grimaced. That was definitely not what she wanted to hear.

It was now officially time for the big push.

"I think he's very sexy," Alexa began.

"That's part of the trouble," Gina grumbled.

Alexa hesitated. Okay, so she'd taken the wrong approach. There was still time. Gina wasn't hanging up so fast.

Alexa quickly racked her brains. It was worth a try.

"He's also a very nice guy, even though most people don't know it," she offered in a serious, earnest tone.

"Really?" Gina asked too quickly. Too loudly.

Bingo.

"Oh, yes," Alexa went on. "He's a generous guy who likes to hide behind a lot of macho stuff." She paused. Actually, she'd never said more than one word to Lucas Baker in her whole life. "I happen to know deep down he's shy."

"Wow," Gina breathed.

Alexa could practically feel Gina's relief. It was terribly satisfying. "Yes, he's — " she was prepared to go on forever if necessary, when suddenly Gina interrupted.

"The problem is, he's invited me to a party at his friend Taylor's house next Saturday night, and I don't want to go alone." Gina paused. "I'm a little nervous."

"Taylor Sheridan?" Alexa asked.

"I . . . I think so." Gina replied. "Why?"

Alexa hesitated. Boy, was Gina heading for a scene. It was so unlike her. So . . . advanced. Still . . .

Suddenly Alexa broke into a smile. It was a perfect idea. The kind she adored. It sparkled. It shimmered. It held the answers.

"Well, I think I could get an invitation to that

party, myself. Would that make you feel better?" Alexa held her breath. She did know a few people who were probably going. She'd just drop by. Give Gina a little confidence, make sure everything was going okay. Then she'd leave.

"Yes!" Gina practically shrieked. "That would make me feel a lot better! None of my friends are going, you know."

"Really?" Alexa asked as if she were completely surprised.

"Yes. In fact, I'd appreciate your not mentioning this to them at all." She paused. "They don't know Lucas like you do."

Alexa could practically hear her smile. It was so rewarding.

"Few people do," Alexa replied, warmth oozing from every pore. Wild horses couldn't drag this Lucas–Gina thing out of her. Not if it meant someone would pull Gina away from Lucas . . . and straight toward Barry.

"Will you be bringing David?" Gina asked sweetly.

Alexa grimaced. She really had to set the record straight. Alexa style. What was the down side? David wasn't about to get swept away by anyone else. She still had plenty of time. "David is definitely into me," she began carefully, "but I am a free bird." She hesitated. "And so is he. . . ." There — that was perfect.

She hadn't exactly said anything, but she'd implied a lot.

"Oh. Fine," Gina replied with disinterest. "Probably Almond Sugar."

"Excuse me?" Alexa asked, a little taken aback.

"You called about what I was baking . . . remember?" Gina asked.

"Oh, yes," Alexa chuckled. "Of course I remember why I called."

She smiled. Phase Four. Roses are red, underway.

12

"Hi, Gina! Feeling okay?" Michelle asked with concern as she joined her friend on the corner Monday morning.

"I'm fine," Gina replied quickly. "Really. It was nothing. Just a cold." She looked down at her books. It was hard lying to Michelle. She didn't deserve it. Not really.

"Well, it wasn't such an exciting party. It was fun watching Alexa in action, but that was about it." Michelle slipped her arm around Gina's shoulder. "We missed you."

Gina nodded. Alexa. Unbelievable. What was happening to her? Had things gotten so crazy that she needed to depend on the most unreliable, untrustworthy person she knew? The one person she'd rather die than cross?

She hugged her books to her chest. Well, actually, yes they had.

"By the way," Michelle continued, "remember I've scheduled for a practice room this afternoon after school. My flute and I will be doing our thing for about half an hour." She smiled at Gina. "You can wait for me, right? You could study or something?"

Gina nodded. "Yes. Okay." Actually, it wasn't okay. She had a lot to do. She worked better at home. Besides, Mara had called last night to invite her to go shopping Wednesday afternoon after school. She was going to be late then. She couldn't afford to get home late now.

Gina looked up at the sky. She could just see herself. All decked out in bright pink leggings. Maybe a bright, loose, deep V-necked sweater and dangling earrings. Mara had said silver would pick up her coloring.

Gina considered her mother. She wouldn't ask so many questions if she got home early today and tomorrow.

She glanced at Michelle. It wasn't going to work.

"Actually, I'm not sure I can wait."

Michelle looked at her with surprise. "But you always do!" she exclaimed.

Gina nodded. That was true. But so what? Couldn't friends be . . . unpredictable?

She looked at Michelle. Apparently not.

"I'll try," she heard herself saying.

"Good." Michelle grinned. "You're great."

Gina nodded. What a nice thing to say.

The question was, how great would she be if she just said no?

Gina sat quietly in the cafeteria, hands folded in her lap, holding her breath.

"I can't believe I have to baby-sit for that fiend Jimmy Marvin again," Vivienne sighed. She took another huge bite of her tuna sandwich. "I need four hands with him."

"Well, maybe one of us can come with you," Margo piped up. "I can't. I have a doctor's appointment. But, maybe . . ." Her eyes trailed around the cafeteria table. They rested on Priscilla. "Maybe she can." She grinned. "Aren't you lucky?!"

Gina considered picking up her tray and walking away.

Priscilla shook her head. "Can't do it. And neither can Michelle. She's got flute practice, and I am doing posters for the social committee. She turned toward Gina. "How about you? You're a great baby-sitter."

Gina felt like dumping her tray in Priscilla's lap.

She hesitated for a long moment. Then she shook her head. "I can't. I'm walking Michelle home, and then I have homework, and . . ."

"Good news!" Vivienne announced. "I don't have to start baby-sitting till four o'clock. You can both meet me there and, in between tying Jimmy to a chair, you can get your work done! Voila! Perfect solution!"

"Not for me," Michelle grinned. "You're on your own. I have to baby-sit Becky. My mother is going out."

Gina looked around the table at her friends.

Why couldn't she say something?

She could feel the anger building. It was almost unbearable.

And at who, exactly, was she angriest. Them or herself?

"I . . . I'm not sure that's going to work for me, either," Gina tried slowly. "I wish it could, but . . ."

"I'll make it work for you," Vivienne interrupted. "Please, Gina. For me? Please."

Gina shrugged. "I'll try . . ." she offered for the second time that day.

"Good," Vivienne replied, sitting back contentedly in her chair. "I can always rely on you." She smiled.

Gina looked down at her chop suey.

What was in this stuff anyway? It looked disgusting.

Almost exactly like the way she felt.

Gina sat in the corner of the library, trying hard to work.

It was almost impossible. She checked her watch for the tenth time since she'd walked in.

Three twenty-five. Only five more minutes to go.

She looked back at her algebra book.

An image of Lucas seemed to smile up at her.

Gina smiled back.

He smelled like . . . the woods.

So earthy.

So free.

She looked around the room at all the familiar faces. Gina smiled. And to think they all thought they knew her. Gina Dumont, the good girl. Nice to everyone. Giving. Kind. Forever reliable.

But they didn't know her. Not really. She had another side. A daring side. A wild side!

She checked her watch again.

Michelle better not be late.

Gina looked down at her red-and-white-striped long-sleeved pullover and jean skirt.

It was a nice look. A Gina look.

But it didn't tell the whole story. Uh-uh.

Gina smiled. Mara was going to help her find that other side. Capture her pizzazz. Lasso her flash.

She checked her watch. She had to go. She felt like a Mexican jumping bean. She just couldn't sit any longer. And that was that.

Gina frowned. Vivienne and Michelle were going to have to manage without her. She started pushing back her chair.

"Hi!" Michelle suddenly whispered in her ear. "Thanks for waiting. Ready?"

Gina popped up so fast, her chair almost toppled over. "Let's go," she whispered back. "Now."

Hurriedly, she moved toward the heavy wood doors, Michelle close behind.

"I didn't mean to be a drag on you," Michelle called after her, an annoyed tone in her voice.

"You're not," Gina replied sharply.

"Vivienne isn't expecting you for another half hour," Michelle called out once more as Gina practically ran ahead of her toward the school's massive front doors. "What's your hurry?"

"Can't go to Viv," Gina called back.

"She's going to be so upset!" Michelle cried out. "Are you sure? She hates that kid."

Gina hesitated. It was true. Viv was going to be very upset. Maybe even angry. She slowed down for a moment. She'd said she would go, hadn't she?

She closed her eyes, trying desperately to remember the conversation. Actually, no. She'd said she would try.

Vivienne had simply thought she would go.

Still . . . she'd left the impression . . .

Gina felt as if she were going to explode.

"Let her baby-sit on her own," she suddenly cried out. "I have a life!"

"What are you talking about? What life?" Michelle cried out. "What's gotten into you?"

Gina hesitated. That was a good question. What had? Her heart was beating quickly now. And was it worth losing her friends? Losing the Crowd?

No. It wasn't. How could it be?

She turned to Michelle and smiled apologetically. "I called my mother. She wants me home right now." She shrugged. "What can I do?"

"Nothing," Michelle smiled sympathetically.

Gina nodded.

Something was definitely going wrong.

Spinning out of control.

All she'd wanted to do was give Gina the perfect a break.

But it was turning into a very nasty, full-time job.

13

Alexa stood in the middle of Leo's, feeling positively electric. All eyes were upon her. She was doing her moonbeam thing.

"And, so, I told him if I'd wanted my baked potato cold, I'd have asked for potato salad!"

Everyone laughed as Alexa felt herself winding up for the punch line. "And would you believe he brought me a small potato salad plate, and then asked for my phone number?!"

"You're kidding," Julie cried out. "In front of your parents?"

Alexa nodded. "You bet." She looked around at all the eager faces smiling enviously, excitedly, admiringly, at her.

Ah, success. Who cared that she'd just made up the story? What counted was they believed it.

Alexa smiled directly at Rick Abel, who was now gazing at her longingly. He wanted her. Her smile brightened. Big deal. Besides, Robin liked him.

"Can I walk you home?" he whispered.

"Alexa!" Mona's familiar voice rang out across the crowded pizza place from the door. "We're here! Let's go!"

Instantly Alexa whirled around. Just in time.

She'd had enough of this, anyway. Rick was no David. That was for sure.

"Sorry. I'll see you soon, Rick," she said softly, turning back around to give him a meaningful smile. Then she scooped up her bag and jacket, blew Julie and Stephanie kisses, and breezed out the door.

A chorus of good-byes chased her onto the sidewalk.

She smiled with satisfaction.

"Sounds like you were having fun in there," Robin commented as they stood outside of Leo's.

"I was," Alexa nodded confidently, snapping shut her jean jacket. "Lots of people to talk to." She took a deep breath and let it out. Then, again, it was nice being out of the spotlight.

Popularity was hard work.

"Let's go in here." Mona tugged at Alexa's sleeve and pointed to the bookstore next door. "There's something I have to pick up."

"Oh, Mona! Every time we walk into a bookstore with you, we end up there for hours!" Robin cried out.

Alexa laughed. "It's true, Mona. I want to go

home." And wait for David to call. Talk a little. She smiled. Send him a kiss or two.

Mona stood her ground. "Well, then, you guys go ahead. I want to go in."

"Oh, great," Robin sighed.

"We'll wait," Alexa grumbled. She peered into the store. It was such a bore. Too quiet. So few people. She was about to announce she'd wait outside, check out the passersby, when another thought popped into her head. She broke into a grin.

She might as well start now.

"You know, Robin, I think I'd like to go in, too," she announced, reaching for the door. "There's something I'd like to look at."

Without waiting for a reply, she breezed in and started walking rapidly through the store. Her eyes scanned the section headings. PSYCHOLOGY, HEALTH, NEW RELEASES. She was near the back of the store. COOKBOOKS, POLITICAL SCIENCE.

Finally she spotted it.

HOBBIES AND CRAFTS.

"Wh-what are you doing?" Robin called from behind as she scurried after Alexa. "What are we looking for?"

Alexa came to a stop in front of the shelf and started running her fingertip along the titles.

She found it almost immediately. *Flower Pressing*. Alexa yanked the book off the shelf and began leafing through it. Page after page had photographs of the prettiest floral designs she'd ever seen.

A soft smile began playing across her lips. "Boy, would I love to do this. . . ." she sighed. She turned back to the table of contents. "Good," she said softly. There were chapters on getting started, diagrams of classic designs, materials, seasonal tips, and more.

"What's good?" Robin said, leaning over Alexa's shoulder. "Pulling flowers apart? What are you, nuts?"

"It's not pulling flowers apart," Alexa snapped. "It's an art form." She paused. "I'm thinking of taking it up in the spring."

She flipped to a page of tiny blossoms arranged in the shape of a heart. She could just imagine making one like it for David. She smiled dreamily. He would be so pleased.

"Well, I'm ready," Alexa said, snapping the book shut. "Where's Mona?"

"Here," Mona called out, walking up the aisle. She held up a book on Greek mythology. "I kind of got into this stuff. I wanted to read more."

Robin chuckled. "You guys are getting very weird on me."

Alexa laughed. "Listen, Robin, do you think I didn't notice that biography of Mozart sitting on your night table the other day?" She paused for effect. "But did I say something? Uh-uh. Not me."

Robin shrugged and looked away. "My mother got it for me."

"SURE!" Mona and Alexa announced in unison as they reached the cashier. All three girls started laughing.

Stepping into the sunlight, Alexa smiled happily.

Everything was going to be perfect.

She'd buy a whole mess of flowers from the flower shop, press them, and present David with her own special gift. A piece of art. Then he'd know for sure how she felt.

He wouldn't even mind how she acted in public.

They'd have an understanding. She adored him. It was just that she had her ways. . . .

"Oh, look who's coming," Robin suddenly whispered, motioning for Alexa to look across the street.

David was walking confidently toward them. Alexa broke into a huge smile. She couldn't help herself. Besides, Mona and Robin knew better than to make too big a deal out of it. She fingered the paper bag clutched in her right hand. She was bursting to show him.

"Hi, Alexa!" a soft, high-pitched voice called out from her left. Alexa whirled around to find Stephanie, Julie, and Stuart Landorf, a ninth-grade friend of Stephanie's, walking toward her.

Alexa looked back toward David.

Okay, so she'd have to play it a little cool. What else was new?

She looked down at the paper bag. If only she'd gotten this sooner. Made one already.

"Hi, David," she said merrily. As if they were the best of pals. Always.

"Hi . . ." he replied a little less brightly. He reached out with one hand and tucked one side of her hair behind her ear.

Alexa continued smiling, but stepped back slightly.

It was the wrong move.

Instantly David started, and moved back as well. He dropped his hand immediately to his side. "So, what are you up to?"

"Oh, nothing, right, girls?" Alexa answered, smiling a little too broadly at Mona and Robin.

"How ya doin', David?" Stuart asked, casually strolling over.

"Fine," David replied, flashing him a friendly smile.

Alexa looked around the group. Her eyes rested on Stephanie, who was now openly looking from David to her and back again. Alexa cleared her throat nervously.

"It's getting a little late," Mona informed everyone.

"Yes, yes, it is!" Alexa exclaimed gratefully. "I've honestly got to get going."

David nodded stonily and promptly started

backing up. "Actually, me, too, everyone. See ya." He didn't even look at her.

Alexa frowned. That was not a good sign. She had to do something. Something meaningful, but noncommittal at the same time.

Something that would keep David from walking away. Forever.

"David," she began awkwardly. "How was your day?" That was good. Just because she cared about his day didn't have to mean they were a major-league couple. Then she smiled at him warmly. It was expected that one could treat a friend with affection.

"Oh, fine," David answered, still backing up. "See ya," he repeated.

Alexa couldn't help herself. She began walking toward him. After all, friends had a right to have a few words alone. . . .

Now, inches away from him, she whispered, "It's good to see you."

"Right," David nodded down at her. "In your dreams."

"Wh-what do you mean?" Alexa stammered. Suddenly she felt a little sick.

"Hey!" David raised both arms in the air. "You've got a right. We're not married." He leaned in close. "We're not even going steady."

Alexa took a step backwards. What did that mean?

He didn't want to go steady? All this time she'd

been trying to make it look like they weren't, when all along they hadn't been, even though she felt as if they were?

Alexa style.

Exactly which one of them was in control, anyway?

Alexa closed her eyes for a long moment. Get hold of yourself. David is just hurt. A little angry. You can get through this. He likes you. You know that.

Alexa moved a touch closer to David. "I'm sorry, I was just surprised to see you and I got uncomfortable." She stared down at the sidewalk.

David nodded. "You sure do get uncomfortable a lot, don't you?" His tone was still tense, but a little less angry. He hesitated. "Look, I didn't mean to snap at you." He paused. "Maybe we could go to the movies Saturday night."

"Okay," Alexa nodded quickly. "Good." She smiled at him encouragingly.

She turned and glanced at her friends. Everyone was looking at them.

It didn't feel good at all. She had to do something.

"So!" she began, louder than necessary, "I'll talk to you then." She smiled broadly, as if she were grinning at her best friend, whirled around, and rejoined the group.

"He's such a nice guy," she said. Alexa smiled right at Stephanie. "Don't you think?"

"Y-yes," Stephanie stammered.

Alexa grinned. Perfect. No one had any idea how she felt.

Impulsively, she turned to glance at David. She waved gaily to him and then quickly looked away.

He didn't look happy.

She was going to have to be on her best behavior Saturday night.

It wasn't until she'd gone another two blocks, lost in thought, that Alexa remembered Gina and the party.

She stopped dead in her tracks.

"What's wrong?" Mona asked with alarm.

Alexa shook her head silently.

What was she going to do?

Gina would die there alone.

And then she'd end up in Barry's arms.

Alexa clutched the paper bag tightly. She was going to have to choose.

Give something up.

She frowned. That was a major problem.

Giving was not her specialty.

14

Wednesday morning Gina woke up with a start ten minutes before her alarm was set to go off. Hurriedly she threw herself out of bed and ran into the shower.

What was she going to do? There was no way she could fit everything in.

She had swim practice.

She had to start work on her book report.

She was supposed to help Margo write the bake sale flyer.

She'd promised her mother she'd be home in time to help with dinner.

Gina grabbed a faded blue towel and began drying herself off.

What did everyone expect?

Why had she promised everything?

All she really wanted to do, all she could think about, was going shopping with Mara. Just for an hour. At three forty-five. Which meant she'd have to leave swim practice early. Which meant there wasn't really any time to do Margo's flyer unless she did it during lunch.

Which was possible. Except she needed that time to study for the science test.

Gina opened her closet and studied its contents. Angrily she shoved hanger after hanger aside. Her white shirt was so prissy. Her black slacks so stiff. Her pink blouse so sweet. Her blue dress so straight.

Everything was wrong.

Nothing fit.

There was trouble in the air. Terrible trouble.

Gina furrowed her brow as she pulled at the sleeve of an old gray sweatshirt. Perfect. The new her.

She glanced down at the closet floor where a stained pair of blue jeans lay crumpled and forgotten.

Defiantly she slipped them on. Gina hesitated for a long moment and then, sighing heavily, she reached for the pink blouse.

The truth was, a person could loosen up just so much in a week.

The moment the bell rang signaling the end of class, Gina flew into the hallway. Anxiously she wove back and forth through the crowd of students.

Margo had to be somewhere.

There was no time to waste. The clock was ticking.

Nearing the wide staircase at the end of the hall, she finally spotted Margo rummaging through her locker.

Gina was upon her in seconds. "Here." She thrust her draft of the flyer into Margo's hand. "I did it during algebra class." She began nervously playing with her hair. "I don't have time for lunch and," she continued, trying to spit the words out as fast as she could, "I can't do it after school." She looked at Margo imploringly. "Okay?"

"But you have to!" Margo cried out. She glanced at the flyer. "It has to say more than this. You promised me we could work on this together."

Gina nodded. She could feel her head beginning to throb. "I know I did, Margo, but I have so much to do, and . . ."

"What do you have to do?" Margo snapped.

"I have to study, I have swim practice, I have . . ."

"You can still take a few minutes to work on this with me," Margo insisted. "You were the one who volunteered."

"Stop it!" Gina snapped suddenly. For a moment she was stunned. She'd never used that tone before. Not to anyone. Well, maybe to Margo. Just the other day.

What was going on?

Margo looked at her wide-eyed.

"I know I promised," Gina rushed on. "But I can't. I'm sorry. I just can't." She looked away.

"What's going on with you, Gina?" Margo persisted. "We've all noticed something's different, but we don't know what it is. Maybe we should have a meeting."

Gina shook her head vehemently. "No way." She cringed. That sounded so awful. Uncaring. Rude, even. "I mean, not now. Please! I'm just so busy," she begged her friend. Gina pointed to the flyer. "I'm sure it will help."

And with that, she turned around and practically flew down the hallway.

This was crazy. She used to be so careful with everyone. So caring . . .

"I can't do everything . . ." she whispered over and over as she moved. "I can't do everything."

She paused in front of the library door.

"And I'm sick of trying."

The words had tumbled out before she had a chance to stop them. Push them back. Ignore them.

Gina took a deep breath.

She was changing.

Gina frowned. Only thing was, she couldn't figure out, into what?

Gina stood in front of the mirror, studying the slinky black jumpsuit and gold chain belt. "I don't know . . ." She looked at Mara dubiously.

"It's fabulous," Mara waved her look away. "You have such a good figure! It makes you look so much older." She handed Gina another belt. This one was made of woven pieces of rough, deep green suede. "Maybe you'll like this better."

Gina slipped off the gold chain belt and tried on the other one. She cocked her head to one side. Actually, they both looked good. She glanced at Mara uncertainly. She felt like her little sister. It was comforting and humiliating all at once.

"I think the gold chain one," Mara said. "It's just the right look for the party."

Gina nodded.

Her eyes moved from studying her own reflection in the mirror to studying Mara. She was wearing torn blue jeans and a scooped-neck navy pullover, a bandanna tied casually around her neck.

She looked utterly cool. Mature. Beautiful.

Gina couldn't help herself. The words fell out of her mouth before she could stop them. "How come you're doing this?" she blurted out. "I . . . I . . . mean, don't you have other things to do? Where's Taylor?"

Mara chuckled. "Actually, I invited you to go shopping with me because I had to go anyway. And I thought it would be fun to change your look." Mara moved her face close to the mirror and, with a fingertip, rubbed away some smudged mascara under her right eye. "I'd also like to be one of those people who selects the wardrobe for actors and actresses on TV. I forget what they're called. Fashion coordinators, or something."

"This has nothing to do with Lucas?" Gina asked, turning halfway around to study the way she looked from behind. Not bad.

"Well . . ." Mara began slowly. "Maybe a little. He did say something to me about you being a little straight." She laughed. "I thought we'd surprise him!" Suddenly she reached up and pulled the front zipper of Gina's jumpsuit down three inches. "Better," Mara proclaimed with a wicked giggle. "So much for straight. Right? You look hot."

Gina nodded. As if straight could certainly no longer apply to her. As if being straight-looking was as foreign to the real her as anyone could get. Gina studied her reflection. Actually, maybe it was. . . . She smiled tentatively.

"I told him you may be a little straight, but you seemed plenty tough to me." Mara giggled again.

Gina smiled. "That's good," she responded. As if Mara had hit the nail right on the head. As if she were exactly right about Gina. Which Gina hoped she was . . .

"So," Mara continued, picking up the dark blue skintight pants she'd selected, "I'd say you look great. It's in your budget. Get it, and let's go get

something to drink at Tanya's Pop down the block.
I'm parched."

And with that, much to Gina's relief, she walked
out of the tiny dressing room. The last thing Gina
wanted to do was allow Mara to see just how
underdeveloped she was.

Just how immature she was.

And, really, just exactly how unhot and un-
tough she really might be.

"Gina?" Mrs. Dumont called out as Gina burst
through the front door.

"Hello, mother," Gina replied. She dropped her
coat and bags on a nearby chair and walked into
the kitchen.

"Your friends called and said you left swim practice early. Why?"

"Because I had studying to do," Gina answered
as she watched her mother neatly slicing carrots.
Not a wrinkle in her pants suit. Not a chip in her
nails. Not a hair out of place.

"I hope this is true, Gina," Mrs. Dumont replied, turning to study her daughter. "I know that
you would never tell me something that is not
true. *Oui?*"

Gina nodded. Of course not.

Gina the perfect? Never.

"Tell me. What were you studying so hard? Per-
haps I can test you later?"

"Science, and no thanks," Gina replied quickly.

"Oh, but I insist," Mrs. Dumont pressed on. "It is a good way to learn."

"But I insist NOT," Gina suddenly blurted out.

There was stunned silence in the room.

"I am not happy with your tone, young lady," her mother said softly. "Not at all. That is not the way a daughter speaks to her mother." She paused. "It is not like you."

Gina looked away. What was like her, anyway?

Did anyone really know?

Her friends thought she was perfect. Straight. Reliable.

Mara thought she was tough. Hot. Free.

And the only thing she knew was that she had to keep going. That something unbelievably exciting was happening to her, and she had to give it room.

Gina grabbed a cucumber and started slicing it feverishly.

"Is something wrong?" Lily Dumont asked, watching her daughter with concern.

Gina looked away. She wasn't sure.

Her friends were furious at her.

She had a date with the fastest guy in Port Andrews' tenth grade.

Her new girlfriend looked like an older sister.

She was counting on Alexa for help.

It sure sounded wrong.

Still, maybe it was right. Necessary.

Like the explosion that was coming any day now.

Gina sighed. The Practically Popular Crowd had had it.

Of course, unbelievably enough, so had she.

She smiled at her mother. "Everything's fine."

Sometimes wishes came true.

15

Alexa could hear the commotion in the front hall as she sat silently on her bed late Thursday afternoon, reviewing her choices. David or Gina. David or Gina. Mimi's excited voice wafted up the staircase into her room.

Alexa rolled her eyes. Mimi's sister had come to meet the family. Oh, joy.

She sighed. Here she was trying to make one of the biggest decisions of her life, and all these happy voices were bouncing off the walls. What a joke.

"Alexa!" her father called out. "Come down and meet someone!" Reluctantly Alexa got to her feet. She was definitely not in the mood for this.

She needed more time. Quiet time. She had to decide what to do Saturday night. And she had to do it soon.

Miserable, she checked her reflection in the mirror, fluffed her hair with her fingers, and started padding toward the circular staircase in her bare feet.

She was halfway down the steps when she came to a complete stop.

"And this is my Lexa baby," Mimi was saying as she reached out toward Alexa. "Pretty little thing, isn't she?"

Mimi's sister nodded enthusiastically. "Yes, she is!"

Alexa nodded slightly.

It was incredible.

She'd never seen anyone quite so fat.

Alexa glanced at Mimi. It was amazing. She didn't even seem to notice. Alexa's eyes traveled over Mimi's tall, trim figure. How could Mimi not notice? How could she not be completely mortified?

"Well," Mr. Craft said warmly, resting his hand lightly on Mimi's shoulder. "I am going to get going. Sarah" — he paused and smiled at Mimi's sister — "it's good to meet you. I'm glad you were able to surprise Mimi early. Have a good dinner." He turned and walked into his den.

Alexa finished descending the stairs and stood awkwardly in the foyer, her eyes glued on Mimi.

"What you starin' at?" Mimi laughed. "Goodness!" She paused. "What's on that mind of yours?"

Alexa shook her head self-consciously and

glanced over at a watercolor hanging on the wall. "Nothing . . ."

"Alexa, Mimi told me you always got yourself some nice-lookin' smart boyfriends!" Sarah laughed. "That so?"

Alexa shrugged. "Sort of." Or at least that was the way it used to be. She glanced at Sarah. Was Mimi actually going to walk around with her? Outside?

"I used to have myself some cute boyfriends, too."

"You did?" Alexa burst out. Instantly horrified, she closed her eyes and grimaced. "Sorry."

Sarah chuckled. "I didn't always look like this. I used to have myself some figure. Isn't that right, Mimi?"

"You better believe it!" Mimi laughed. "I used to be jealous." She smiled warmly at her sister and then glanced at Alexa. "You sure you're okay? You look like you're floatin' away."

"No . . ." Alexa shook her head. "I'm okay."

"Fine," Mimi smiled. "We're on our way out to some nice place for dinner."

Alexa gave Sarah a long, lingering look.

How was Mimi doing it?

Sure, Sarah wasn't exactly obese, but she looked so . . . so . . . huge. The last place she ought to be seen was stuffing her face at a restaurant.

Alexa glanced at Mimi. What would people think of her?

Alexa shuddered.

"Well, I can see you've got your mind someplace else," Mimi broke into her thoughts, "so I believe we'll just be on our way."

"Actually, Mimi," Alexa suddenly interjected. "I would like to talk with you alone just for a sec, if that's okay."

It was just too much to believe. Somewhere, somehow, Mimi had to be dying.

"Thought so," Mimi nodded knowingly. " 'Scuse us, Sarah." And with that, she put down her bag on the entrance table and walked through the hallway door toward the kitchen.

"So?" She leaned against the inside of the kitchen door and folded her arms across her chest. "What's up?"

Alexa began chewing on her lower lip, saying nothing.

"Lexa, baby, I can't just stand here . . ."

"Your sister is very fat," Alexa blurted out.

"Yes. She is," Mimi replied curtly. "Had a rough life. I think she eats to make herself feel better." She paused. "Is that all you have to say?"

Alexa nodded. She could see David now. His physique that was a little too thin. His nose that was a little too large.

"You're going to a restaurant, though?" Alexa asked.

Mimi furrowed her brow. "Well, yes. She's fat, but she still needs to eat somethin' . . ." Mimi shook her head. "What's this all about? This isn't what you needed to talk to me about, is it? What are . . ."

"Aren't you embarrassed?!" Alexa finally managed. "How could you walk into a public place with her?"

Mimi unfolded her arms and pointed to herself. "Embarrassed? Me? Why?" She placed both hands on her hips. "I'm not fat, and I don't think I like where you're heading."

"But . . . but . . ."

"But what?"

"Don't you think people are going to think you're sort of weird being with someone who looks so . . ."

"I don't know. Do I look weird to you?"

"No," Alexa shrugged. "Never mind." She looked away. "Have a nice dinner." Mimi didn't understand. She was so glad to see her sister, she couldn't think straight.

Mimi straightened her shoulders and lifted her chin. "I most certainly will have a nice dinner." She paused. "But let me say something, Lexa, baby. Look at me first."

Alexa turned back to Mimi reluctantly.

"I am Mimi Summers. I am a nice, funny, smart person. And I'm goin' to stay that way, no matter who I'm with. Besides, I don't worry much 'bout what people say concernin' the people I see. You know why?"

Alexa shook her head.

"Because I don't have a choice."

"Th-that's not true," Alexa sputtered. Sure, she had a choice. Just like Alexa did. David, or some other real cute guy.

"Sure it is. Because I want to be happy, and I'm happiest bein' with people who make me feel good. Not look good."

"But . . . but . . . don't you care about what people think of you?"

"Sure I do." Mimi nodded. "I just think they ought to decide that by who I am. Not who I'm with."

"But that's not how it works," Alexa shook her head sadly. "Not at school, anyway."

Mimi smiled sympathetically. "You gonna let your life be taken over by what your friends think of your friends?"

Alexa shrugged. That was the problem. She couldn't decide.

Mimi cupped Alexa's chin in her hand. "Listen, Lexa, baby. Today I'm goin' with my sister to some nice restaurant. And I'm goin' to walk in that door, and I'm goin' to see people look at her. I might even see 'em whisper. But I'm goin' to take my seat, and have a nice dinner. And I'm goin' to feel bad for all those folks, too."

"Bad?" Alexa asked incredulously. "Why?"

" 'Cause they don't know my sister, who happens to be one of the best people I know. That's why. Besides, bein' fat isn't the worst thing. Some people think fat is beautiful, you know." Mimi chuckled. "Sarah's got herself a handsome husband."

She pushed open the kitchen door and turned to settle a serious look on Alexa. "And don't think I don't know David's behind all this. And here's what I'm gonna say 'bout that. You just go right on likin' that boy. 'Cause if they're smart, your friends are goin' to figure out maybe you know somethin' they don't." She smiled at Alexa warmly. "And if they're not smart, who needs 'em? Believe you me. That's the only way you're goin' to get happy." And with that, she walked through the door.

Alexa pulled out a chair, sat down, and rested her head in her hands.

Happy. Yes. David made her happy.

But it wasn't that simple.

Mimi didn't understand one very important thing.

Alexa was too afraid to be happy.

Alexa was too afraid to be anything but utterly, and absolutely the most envied girl at Port Andrews Junior High.

David just didn't help the cause.

And, Gina, well, she stood to ruin it altogether.

16

Gina climbed out of the swimming pool, waved at her coach, and picked up her towel. She looked around at her teammates and smiled.

"You clocked good times today," she grinned at Mariko Tanaka. "I wish mine were as good."

"Yours were good, too," Mariko smiled back. "You were faster a few days ago, and you'll be faster again!" She patted Gina on the shoulder and headed for the locker room.

Gina whisked off her swim cap and shook out her long, light brown hair. Actually, in many ways, she'd never been faster, she thought to herself with a smile. An icy feeling raced up her spine. Gina wrapped the towel more tightly around her body. It didn't help.

Okay, so she was nervous. The party was in two days, and her old friends wouldn't be there.

Gina began heading toward the locker room. She shivered once again. Of course, she had new friends now.

Reaching the entrance door, she swung it open hurriedly and stepped inside.

But that was as far as she got.

Her eyes settled on the wooden bench in the small front room leading into the locker room . . . where Margo, Michelle, Vivienne, and Priscilla now sat stiffly, waiting for her.

"Wh-what's wrong?" Gina stammered, looking from one girl to the next. She wrapped her arms around herself. "I wasn't expecting you. . . ."

She moved aside quickly so the rest of the swim team could file through the double doors leading to the locker room.

"We know that," Vivienne snapped. "But you have been utterly unavailable. We thought this was the only way."

Gina nodded and looked quickly away.

Funny. She had no desire to talk. No desire to do or say anything. It felt like the calm before the storm.

It felt dark.

What was the matter with her? Here they were, wanting to talk, and all she wanted them to do was leave. Her friends.

Or were they really her friends?

Gina looked back at them.

Actually, she wasn't sure. They were cornering her, and it was making her angry. Very angry.

"We were hoping you'd explain to us how come

you've been acting so funny lately," Michelle began. "You're usually so much more . . ."

"Agreeable?" Gina finished stiffly. Instantly she looked away, focusing on a piece of chipped paint on the opposite wall.

"Well . . . no . . . not that," Michelle went on quietly, clearly straining not to raise her voice. "Just, well, honestly . . . reliable."

"Are you angry at us about something?" Priscilla asked, drumming her fingertips on her black art portfolio.

Gina shook her head. She was and she wasn't. And, anyway, no matter what the truth was, for some reason she didn't want to discuss it now.

"Well, you're thinking something, and The Practically Popular Crowd would like to know what it is," Vivienne insisted, standing up. "You're acting like a crazy person lately, and it's getting on my nerves." She pointed at Margo. "Also hers."

Gina sucked in her breath. She looked from one face to the next. No one said a word.

The moment had come. Who knew? Maybe she'd been asking for it all along. Pushing for it. Aching to see if she could manage.

Gina narrowed her eyes and squared her shoulders.

"I don't care," she said quietly, looking at each girl one at a time.

"Excuse me?" Margo asked, leaning slightly back as if someone had tried to push her over. She giggled nervously. "What is this? *Candid Camera?*"

"I said," Gina began again, louder this time, "I don't care."

"Very nice," Vivienne replied sharply. "What a pal."

"You don't mean that, do you?" Priscilla asked incredulously. She had stopped drumming on her portfolio and was now staring at Gina, wide-eyed.

Gina looked down at the tiled floor.

She wasn't sure if she meant it.

She was positive, however, that right now, at this moment, she felt it. Intensely.

"Well, before I get up and walk out, would you like to tell me why?" Vivienne continued. "I mean, I feel like I'm in the Twilight Zone."

Gina took a deep breath and looked at the ceiling.

What difference did it make what they thought? She'd blown it already, anyway.

"Lucas Baker . . ." she murmured softly.

"What?" Margo yelped. "Did you say Lucas Baker?"

Gina nodded. "We're going out."

"You're not," Priscilla shook her head. "I can't believe that."

"Why?" Gina said, staring at her icily. "Because perfect Barry is more my type?"

Priscilla hesitated. "Well, I thought you liked him."

"Why?" Gina persisted. She could feel the anger beginning to bubble crazily to the surface. "I never said I did. NEVER!"

"Well, you never said you didn't, either!" Priscilla snapped back. "Did you?"

This time, Gina hesitated. No, she hadn't. But that didn't matter. That wasn't the point. And even if it were, right now she didn't want it to be.

Right now, for some completely insane reason, Gina just wanted to explode. Shake everything up. Cause an earthquake. Stir up a hurricane.

"I'm not what you think I am!" Gina cried out. "I'm wilder than you know. I'm not so perfect. I do risky things!" As if to illustrate the point, Gina twirled around three times until the room began to spin.

She stopped. "And I like it this way."

"I feel like I don't know you anymore," Viv responded stonily.

"You don't," Gina nodded.

She closed her eyes for a brief moment. Actually, she didn't know herself much, either, these days.

"Frankly, Gina, I think you're nuts to go out with Lucas," Margo said softly. "He's way too much for you."

Gina whirled around and glared at Margo. "How

117

do you know that? How do you know I can't handle him?"

"Okay! Maybe I don't!" Margo cried out. "I'm a moron! All right?" She scrambled to her feet. "I don't want to listen to this garbage anymore. You're being mean and rotten and I don't understand a word you're saying, and I'm not even sure I care anymore, either." She picked up her book bag. "I'm leaving."

"Well . . . wait . . . Margo," Priscilla began, reaching out to stop Margo. She turned toward Gina. "How about if we try to talk again on Saturday night. We're all meeting at Margo's to do some baking."

Gina shook her head. It was bizarre. It was almost fun.

Shocking everyone.

Looking out for Gina. The new Gina. The independent Gina.

"Priscilla, I have no time Friday to tutor. Not if I'm going to bake for the sale and do my homework and have a tennis lesson and still have time to see Lucas Saturday night." She shrugged with an unapologetic smile. "Sorry."

"You said you'd help me," Priscilla practically hissed.

"No, you said I *had* to," Gina protested. "There's a difference."

"What are you, my slave? You couldn't have said no?"

"No! I couldn't! You kept pushing, and pushing . . ." Gina cried out, her voice beginning to crack. She looked around. "That's all you do! Push!"

"I see, it's my fault," Priscilla said, bending down to pick up her portfolio. "That's it, I'm out of here."

Gina watched as each of her friends headed toward the door.

Go, a voice inside her head cried out. *See if I care.*

Suddenly, she felt herself beginning to tremble.

Impulsively, she reached out and grabbed Michelle's hand. "You know," she whispered hoarsely, "you guys know, I always say yes to everything. You should have stopped asking."

Michelle gently pulled her hand away.

"You should have spoken up, anyway."

Gina shook her head. "I couldn't."

Michelle settled an icy glare on Gina. "You mean until now."

"Well, you don't like the real me, do you?" Gina asked defiantly. She raised her voice and repeated the question. "You guys don't like me when I'm not doing what you want, do you?"

All four girls turned to stare at her with a mixture of confusion, hurt, and anger, and one by one they filed quietly out the door.

"I thought so . . ." Gina murmured. She looked around the almost empty locker room.

She was on her own now.

She leaned back against the wall.

Maybe this was the way it was supposed to be.

Now she could really fly.

Discover herself.

Be everything she'd always wanted.

Gina smiled a little too broadly and took off her wet bathing suit. It was a good feeling. Kind of like a bird in flight. She began drying off with a fresh towel. An uncaged tiger. Suddenly, she stopped.

Memories of The Practically Popular Crowd came crashing down upon her. One after another. Endlessly. Margo's diet problems. Michelle's little sisters. Priscilla's ever-present sketchpad. Vivienne's tough-guy routine that hid so much insecurity. An avalanche of thoughts. The whispering of romantic secrets. The absolute confidences. The unshakable togetherness.

Gina placed her head in her hands and burst into tears.

Breaking free meant everything.

But the price. Did it have to be so terribly, awfully, high?

17

Alexa sat down at her white-laced dressing table Saturday afternoon and smiled serenely into the mirror. Maybe, in just a few more hours, she and David would be alone. Talking. Holding hands. Looking into each other's eyes.

It could be so lovely.

So . . . romantic.

"Hark, what light through yonder window breaks . . ." Alexa recited contentedly as she snapped on the makeup lights that encircled the mirror. " 'Tis Alexa . . ." She smiled.

She closed her eyes for a moment, imagining David's smile as she greeted him at the door. Pulling over her lavender makeup basket, she surveyed the contents carefully.

Yes, it could be wonderful.

Unless she decided to go with Gina to the party.

Alexa sighed heavily.

Four hours to go, and she still had no idea what she was doing. Things were an incredible mess.

Alexa covered her face with her hands. What was most important? What? David, despite what everyone thought, or keeping Gina away from Barry because of what everyone would think?

Alexa sighed miserably. Operation Invisible Love wasn't working. Something had gone terribly wrong.

She was about to pick up a tube of dark blue mascara when the phone rang.

"Alexa?" Gina's soft voice seemed to float across the wire.

Alexa took a deep breath. "Yeah. Hi." She began tapping her foot nervously on the thick lavender rug. "I was just going to call you," she lied.

"Oh, well," Gina continued breathlessly, "I just wanted to know when you were going to pick me up."

Alexa hesitated.

Decision time.

The truth was, she hadn't intended to call Gina. The truth was, she had made no firm plan about how to handle this with David, either. She had just sort of hoped it would all work itself out.

Like things usually did.

Without her giving up a thing. Darn.

She checked her watch. Maybe there was still time. . . .

"Actually . . ." Alexa leaned forward and flicked a dark speck of something off her cheek.

Actually, there was no more time. The truth was, she had to say something. This was it. Alexa closed her eyes, her mind spinning.

"Hello?" Gina asked. "Are you there?"

"I thought maybe you could go on your own," Alexa finally suggested softly. "Is that okay?"

"You mean, walk in by myself?" Gina asked tentatively.

Alexa paused. Actually, no. That wasn't what she'd meant. But it certainly was easier to agree. "Kind of," Alexa replied carefully.

"I hadn't really wanted to," Gina paused. "Of course, maybe Mara could pick me up on the way. I'm sort of embarrassed to ask, though."

"Oh. Perfect idea," Alexa exclaimed a little too loudly. Actually, she had no idea who Mara was. "She's a very nice person. Really."

"When will you get there?" Gina asked anxiously. "Maybe we could at least get there around the same time. . . ."

Alexa cocked her head to one side and ran a brush through her hair, watching as it glistened in the light.

"Early, I hope," she replied simply. And she did hope, too. That wasn't a lie. She just had a feeling it wouldn't happen.

Alexa nervously began lining up her eyeshadows.

There was no way out.

Gina was going to freak out when she got there, blow it with Lucas, and fly straight into Barry's arms.

She just knew it.

On the other hand, if she cancelled on David, he would simply walk away. He was that close.

She could feel it.

Her eyes came to rest on a penny sitting on the tabletop. Impulsively she threw it into the air. Heads, David. Tails, Gina.

"I'm so glad you're coming to the party," Gina continued eagerly. "I know it seems silly, but I'm just not used to Lucas's crowd."

Alexa caught the penny. For the longest moment she considered just tossing it aside. Throwing it in her drawer. Not looking.

"Not used to them, I know," Alexa mumbled absentmindedly.

Then, very slowly, she opened her hand.

Heads.

"So, I'll see you," Alexa said softly.

"You, too," Gina answered a little too quickly. A little too anxiously. "Soon, I hope."

Alexa nodded. Even she couldn't bear to say one more word.

Early Saturday evening Gina walked into her bedroom, closed the door, and locked it. She didn't really have to. Her parents had just left to have dinner with friends.

But she did anyway.

It added to the secrecy. The excitement.

It was costume time.

Pulling open her closet, she rummaged around until her hand grasped the shopping bag she'd stuck way in the back in the left-hand corner. Slowly she drew it out of the closet and placed it on her bed. Taking off her clothes, Gina slipped into a bathrobe, unlocked her door, and stepped into the small bathroom outside her room.

She turned on the water and stepped into the shower.

She closed her eyes.

This was going to be an extraordinary night.

A kind of new beginning.

Sure, she felt bad about her old friends. Yes, she'd cried about it. But, look, people outgrow friends sometimes. It wasn't anyone's fault. No. Not at all. These things just happen.

Gina grabbed for the conditioning shampoo.

The important thing was that she'd told them. She'd gotten it out. And now she was free to be whomever she wanted.

Gina smiled, her eyes still closed.

Lucas's girl.

Her smile lessened just a bit.

It didn't feel exactly right.

But why not?

Gina Dumont could be a wild and crazy girl.

And she still had friends. Like Mara. And Alexa.

For a moment, Gina frowned. Had it been her imagination? Alexa sounded funny on the phone. As if she were thinking something she wasn't saying. Gina began chewing on her lower lip. Luckily, Mara had agreed to meet her earlier.

But, really, that didn't help much. She needed Alexa badly. It wasn't a good feeling. Counting on Alexa was a little like staring at a storm cloud and convincing yourself it wouldn't rain.

Gina stepped out of the shower, wrapped herself up in a large, light blue bath sheet, and picked up her toothbrush.

Well, even Alexa deserved a little trust. Didn't she?

Besides, no matter what, her first really big date as the new Gina Dumont was waiting. . . .

What a terrific thought that was.

She caught a glimpse of herself in the mirror.

So how come she wasn't smiling?

18

"I had a wild day," David chuckled, squeezing Alexa's hand affectionately. "I got lassoed into helping my dad finish up the wood shelving in the basement."

"Was it hard work?" Alexa asked, looking up into his big blue eyes. She smiled. She could just see him. A hammer in one hand, a bunch of nails in the other.

He had probably looked adorable.

If only other girls had seen him that way.

Quickly, for about the third time in five minutes, Alexa craned her neck to look down the growing line of people waiting to enter the theater.

So far, so good. Sure, a few familiar faces. But no one that mattered. She squeezed David's hand. Maybe they'd get away with seeing no one. It was possible. Especially if they went straight back to her house after the film.

"Are you expecting someone?" David asked, peering down the line just as she had.

Alexa blanched, and then focused intently on the ticket booth straight ahead. "Don't be silly," she replied humorlessly. "Of course not." She began playing with the buttons on her jacket.

Still holding Alexa's hand, David took a small step away, turned, and looked into her eyes. "What's with you? You're awful jumpy again."

Alexa began fidgeting with her sterling star dangle earrings. "What do you mean?" she asked wide-eyed, feigning confusion.

It wasn't difficult.

"Never mind," David shrugged. "Just a feeling I have . . . ." He, too, began looking straight ahead.

You're losing him, a soft voice inside her head whispered. Do something.

Alexa impulsively leaned her head against his right shoulder. Instantly David reached over with his hand and began stroking her hair.

For a moment she forgot herself.

Alexa smiled. The feelings. They were so cozy and warm.

She allowed herself to enjoy them for about ten seconds and then lifted her head. Abruptly.

She bent down to scratch her ankle and then quickly, ever so secretly, twisted her head around just a bit to check the line.

Good. Still no one worth worrying about.

Straightening up, Alexa turned to gaze at

David, who was studying her with an annoyed expression on his face.

"So. Have you found who you're looking for yet?" he asked, both hands now crammed firmly in his pockets. "Maybe I should have brought my binoculars?"

Alexa opened her mouth to speak.

But nothing came out.

This was ridiculous. She had to get a grip. Who cared if she ran into someone?! This was real romance. Remember what Mimi said. What mattered was being happy.

Suddenly, Alexa stepped toward David and slipped her arm around his waist. "I don't need binoculars," she grinned. "Just you."

"Okay," David smiled back, slipping his arm around her shoulders. "That's more like it."

Alexa nodded. Yes, it was. Absolutely.

She could feel her resolve taking shape.

Now, if she could only stick with the feeling for more than ten seconds at a time.

Gina stood in front of the mirror and considered her look.

The black slinky jumpsuit was ultra flattering. It made her look slim. Tall and graceful. Tentatively, Gina reached up and fingered the zipper that was now pulled all the way up.

She tugged at it slightly. Then a bit more.

Unbelievable.

She didn't look like Gina Dumont, goody two shoes, at all.

Not one bit.

She giggled. And to think she had been cool all the time!

Gina leaned into her makeup mirror and double-checked the blue eye shadow. It was a bit heavier on one eye than the other. She grabbed a Q-tip and evened it out.

Perfect.

Her friends would not believe it if they saw her now.

Gina frowned. Make that her ex-friends.

She checked her watch. Mara would be there any second. She twirled one more time and, seconds later, the doorbell rang.

Grabbing her small red shoulder bag, Gina flicked off the light in her room and dashed downstairs. Opening the hall closet, she grabbed her navy blue jacket, flung a bright red scarf around her neck, and checked herself one more time in the hall mirror.

No question about it. She was looking good.

Gina opened the door.

Mara, wearing a bright pink bomber jacket, was standing on the doorstep with a girl Gina had never seen before.

In fact, she wasn't quite sure she was just a girl at all. She looked about eighteen.

"Hi, Gina," Mara sang out cheerily. She pointed to the girl. "This is Deborah. A friend of mine." She paused. "Deborah, this is Gina."

Gina smiled at her uncertainly. Talk about cool.

Deborah was wearing a short, cranberry-colored leather jacket over a pair of dark green stirrup pants. Her thick, very long, dark hair hung almost to her waist and almost completely hid her large gold hoop earrings from which dangled a multitude of tiny charms.

Self-consciously, Gina glanced down at the bright red scarf she had wound around her neck only moments ago. Why had she done that? It was so . . . goofy. Juvenile.

"Well," Mara continued. "Are you ready?" She swiveled her hips. "This is going to be a fun night! Let me tell you!"

Deborah broke into a smile and casually tossed her hair back over her shoulders.

Gina started. It was an Alexa move. Only on Alexa, it just looked sort of conceited. On Deborah, it almost looked scary.

She hesitated.

"Gina? Are you with us?" Mara reached out and tugged at Gina's arm. "Can we go now? Do you want us to say hi to your parents?"

Gina shook her head. "No . . . no . . . they're not home."

"Oh, well, then you're the one who should be having the party!" Deborah cackled. Once again, she threw her hair back over her shoulders.

Gina laughed, as if she thought that was very funny. Which she didn't. Not at all.

"Well, I suppose we should go," she said quietly. She began fishing around in her bag for the housekeys. Her fingers found them. She didn't pull them out.

Something didn't feel right. Just ten minutes ago, she'd felt as if she'd discovered a whole new self. But now . . .

"Gee, Gina, you don't sound too excited," Mara frowned. "Something happen with Lucas I don't know about? Last I heard, he was really gone on you!"

Gina looked up at Mara thoughtfully.

That was true. And she was crazy about him, too. Kind of.

So she didn't look as old as Deborah, or as sophisticated as Mara. So what? She could fit. She was somewhat sure of it.

She looked from Mara to Deborah and smiled broadly. "Well, what are we waiting for?" she asked with forced brightness. As casually as possible she removed the red scarf and tossed it on the table. Then Gina pulled the keys from her bag, stepped outside, and double-locked the door behind her.

She took a deep breath, let it out, and checked her watch. Maybe Alexa would be there when they arrived.

"I think Lucas is probably at Taylor's already, Gina," Mara commented as they walked down the steps. "Won't that be great?"

Gina cleared her throat. "Yes, it will," she managed. Actually, that wasn't far from the truth. She was excited about seeing Lucas.

It's just that she wished she were seeing him someplace else.

Like at Michelle's house.

Or in the daytime.

Gina shivered just a little as they made their way down the street. Okay. So she didn't feel real comfortable. So it felt a little like playing a part. She was used to that. She was used to playing the part of Ms. Goody Gina. So now she had a new role. A more exciting one.

She'd grow into it. She had to.

After all, she had no place else to go.

Alexa sat, one hand clasped tightly in David's, watching the previews. She took another sip of her diet Coke and leaned back against the chair.

This was the most cooled out she'd been with David in ages.

Of course, little wonder.

The theater was dark, and they were sitting off in a corner.

"This is nice," she whispered to David.

"You think so, huh?" he whispered back. For a

moment he turned and stared lovingly into her eyes, and then lightly he touched his lips to hers.

Alexa felt her body tingle excitingly. She gently rested her hand on his cheek as a signal for him to continue the kiss.

She could have stayed that way forever.

"I'd love some popcorn," David suddenly whispered, his lips just a millimeter from hers.

"That's very romantic," Alexa giggled. "That's what you were thinking about? Popcorn?"

David chuckled. "I'm hungry. What can I say?"

Alexa grinned. "Me, too. Go get some. I'll share."

"Large popcorn coming up," David replied cheerfully as he stood up. He turned to walk up the aisle.

Alexa nestled back in her seat and closed her eyes. If only things could be this easy. And maybe they could. Maybe she could let everyone know. She just needed a little more time. Maybe at some point soon she could actually . . .

"Alexa . . . Alexa . . ." she heard David's voice whispering to her in the dark. "Guess who I see sitting by the door!"

Alexa froze.

"Alexa," David was gently tapping her shoulder.

"Who?" Alexa whispered back. Softly. Miserably.

"Stephanie, Julie, Pete, and some guy I don't know." He paused. "I'm going to say hello."

Alexa nodded. "Do that."

"Wanna come?" he asked, extending his hand.

Alexa shook her head. "Not now." She slid down lower into her seat. "I'm a little tired."

"Be right back," David nodded. "Maybe we'll have sodas with them afterwards."

Alexa turned toward him in the darkness. "Maybe," she whispered.

"Is everything okay?" David asked.

Alexa hesitated. Thankfully, the theater was almost black.

If it hadn't been, he wouldn't have needed to ask.

He'd have seen the look on her face.

He'd have known that nothing, absolutely nothing, was okay at all.

"Yes. Everything's fine," she answered softly. Once again, she closed her eyes.

She'd run out of time.

It was tonight . . . or never.

19

Gina followed Mara and Deborah into Taylor's house and immediately busied herself with her coat. She unbuttoned it slowly. She removed it casually. She folded it over her arm. She asked where to put it.

She wanted to look busy. Involved. Relaxed.

She wanted Alexa.

The party was already very noisy. Very intimidating.

"Hello, there," Lucas drawled in a low voice, coming up from behind her. "I've been waiting for you." He waved an arm toward the living room. "My friends," he said proudly.

Gina smiled up at him. In a way, he looked like a movie star.

An outlaw. A guy on the run. Rugged and handsome.

Streetwise. Cool.

Like he traveled on a motorcycle.

She turned to survey the party.

People were dancing. Slow and close.

"Shall we?" Lucas asked with an inviting sparkle in his eye.

Gina hesitated. Not yet, she wanted to say. Let's talk first. She was about to suggest they get something to drink, when Lucas slipped his arm around her waist and started leading her toward the center of the living room.

She couldn't resist.

She didn't entirely want to.

The old Gina was becoming a dim memory.

Placing her arms around his neck, Gina felt his strong arms encircle her waist. She leaned her head on his shoulder and took a long deep breath, letting it out slowly and happily.

"I'm glad you came," Lucas whispered in her ear.

Gina smiled. "Me, too." She looked around the room. It didn't exactly look like the parties she was used to. More people were necking. There were a few beer cans around. A couple of people were smoking cigarettes.

But nothing she couldn't handle.

She hoped.

"You look beautiful tonight," Lucas continued. "Very sexy."

Gina smiled into his shoulder. So, she'd finally done it. She'd gotten rid of Ms. Goody Two Shoes. And she'd let the secret Gina out. A little wild. A little crazy. A free spirit. This was much more exciting. She hugged Lucas ever so slightly. He really wasn't too much for the new her. In fact, in a way, he was her savior.

Her hero.

What a fool she'd been.

Gina closed her eyes.

And then his right hand began to move.

Just slightly at first. It traveled up her back to her neck and then down once more. Then back up again, slowly.

It began pressing her toward him. Firmly. Deliberately.

Gina could feel her entire body begin to tense. She tried, ever so gently, to push away from him. Just a little bit.

But he didn't seem to notice.

Or, he didn't seem to want to let her.

Either way, she didn't like it.

She picked her head up slightly and scanned the room.

Where was Alexa? She needed Alexa.

"What's wrong?" Lucas whispered in her ear. "Am I making you nervous?"

Gina shook her head slightly and tried to will her body to relax. "No . . . no," she murmured.

Calm down, the voice inside her head instructed. It's just new. You're not used to acting . . . older.

The music was over then, and Gina pulled more firmly away from Lucas's grasp. His arms remained around her waist. For a moment, she gazed up into his intense dark green eyes. He smiled down at her and, then, suddenly, before she knew what was happening, he dipped his head and began kissing her neck.

Soft, gentle kisses.

Gina didn't know what to do. Where to look. There were people everywhere. No one seemed to notice. But still.

Was she supposed to just stand there? Be quiet? Giggle? Kiss him back? Somehow? But where?

"Hey, you two," a voice from right next to them cried out. "That's what the back room is for!" Gina turned to find Taylor standing inches away. He thrust a beer can toward her. "Here you go. Enjoy yourself."

Gina started to reach for the can, and then suddenly dropped her hand to her side. "No, thanks," she whispered.

"Huh?" Taylor said, still extending the can. "I can't hear you."

"I said maybe later," Gina replied a little louder this time. She watched helplessly as Lucas took the can instead, popped off the top, and began to chug it down.

Hearing the front door open once again, Gina whirled around. Alexa had to be coming any moment. She had to be.

Suddenly, she began to shiver.

"Hey? Are you cold?" Lucas asked, putting his

arm protectively around her shoulders. He laughed. "I could warm you up, you know."

"I know," Gina smiled slightly. She stood stiffly by his side and kept her eyes glued to the door.

This wasn't working.

She'd thought it might. But it wasn't.

She'd wanted it to. But it couldn't.

She could feel the tears beginning to form.

She wasn't wild and crazy.

And she wasn't Ms. Goody Two Shoes.

She looked down at her slinky black jumpsuit.

The truth was, she had absolutely no idea who she was.

She only knew one thing absolutely.

She wanted to leave.

Alexa sat perfectly still, eyes riveted to the screen, as if no movie had ever been so thrilling. But she was seeing nothing. Hearing nothing.

She was vaguely aware of David's arm, which was draped casually over the back of her seat. But, otherwise, her mind was several rows back.

On Stephanie, and Pete, and Julie, and whomever.

He was probably handsome, whoever he was.

Julie wouldn't be caught dead with anything less.

Alexa closed her eyes. And here she was. Dead meat.

If there was only some way to get out of there

without having to actually talk to them. Sure, David probably already told them he was with her. But if they didn't see them . . . if they didn't see David with his arm around her . . . nuzzling her . . . acting as if they were on a date . . . she could always explain it away.

"We're pals! He was dying to see this movie, and so was I." Or, "It was just a friend thing. We like movies." Or, better yet, "David's fun to spend time with, but boy did I have a hot time the other day with . . ."

Alexa frowned.

Actually, she hadn't had a particularly exciting time with anyone else lately. How could she have? She only really liked David.

Suddenly, her eyes lit upon the exit sign off to her right. She turned. There were another two off to her left.

That was it.

Probably the theater would open one of them.

She'd say, "Come on, David. Let's go this way. It's faster."

No one would ever see them.

No one would ever know.

At least not until the time she was ready to tell them.

On the one hand, it seemed just around the corner.

On the other, it felt like a zillion years away.

20

"Where's the phone?" Gina asked casually as she finally pulled away from Lucas. His arm dropped heavily to his side.

"Try the kitchen," Lucas replied, pointing in the general direction. "Who you calling?" He grinned. "Mom?"

Gina shook her head and looked quickly away.

It was humiliating. It was showing after all.

Ms. Straight rides again.

"A friend," she murmured, brushing past him.

"Hi, Gina!" Mara called out as she entered the kitchen. She was busy pouring a fresh bag of potato chips into a wooden bowl. "I'm feelin' fine." She wiggled her hips. "How 'bout you?"

Gina smiled. "Just great," she answered loudly. She spotted the phone hanging on the wall next to the fridge. Quickly picking it up, she dialed Alexa's number and covered her other ear with her hand.

"Hello," Alexa's housekeeper, Mimi, answered the phone.

"Yes," Gina spoke softly, but urgently. "Is Alexa still there?"

Mimi hesitated. "Why, no. Who is this?"

"Gina Dumont."

"Oh, Gina, hi, darlin'. No, she isn't. She left a good hour or so ago. Why?"

"An hour!" Gina cried out more loudly than she'd intended. Immediately she softened her voice. "But she's not here yet."

"Where?" Mimi said, a little nervously now. "You at the movies, too?"

"Movies? What movie?" Gina answered, feeling herself growing more frantic by the minute.

"She went with David to the movies."

"But . . . but . . . she was supposed to be here!" Gina cried out softly. "At Taylor's."

"At whose?" Mimi answered. "Are you okay, Gina? You sound scared or somethin'."

"No . . . no . . . I'm okay," Gina replied quickly.

"Maybe you got your dates wrong," Mimi offered helpfully.

"Yeah . . . maybe," Gina replied softly, shaking her head.

How could she have been so foolish.

So completely trusting.

She looked up at the kitchen clock. Nine o'clock.

Too late to walk home by herself. Too early to ask Lucas to take her. She stared down at the floor for a long moment.

"Hello . . . hello . . ." Mimi's voice traveled across the line. "Are you still there? Do you want me to give Alexa a message?"

"Huh?" Gina stammered. "No . . . no . . . it's okay." Numb, she continued holding the receiver for a long moment, and then finally, she hung it up.

Slowly, Gina walked back into the living room.

"Hey, Gina," Mara called out.

Gina turned around in the direction of Mara's voice. She was sitting on Taylor's lap on the sofa. Lucas was sitting next to them, beckoning to Gina.

Gina began moving toward them.

There was nothing else to do. She was trapped.

She brushed past a couple who were kissing so passionately, it was almost embarrassing.

In fact, it *was* embarrassing. Gina cringed.

Lucas was smiling broadly now, patting his lap as if to say, "Come on over. This is your seat."

Gina smiled back. It didn't make a difference, though.

A deep and painful sob was straining her chest.

How could Alexa have done this! Left her here! On her own! With these people!

Gina tried to take a deep breath, but she couldn't.

She was too angry. Too upset.

She was almost there now.

"Glad you're back," she heard Lucas say.

"How's it going?" she heard Taylor ask in her direction as his hand traveled up and down Mara's back.

And, then, suddenly, Gina simply turned around.

It was as if she flipped a switch.

On, and then off.

It was that simple.

Quickly, she rushed to the kitchen and reached for the phone.

She closed her eyes.

They'd help her. They had to. Look at all the times she'd helped them. Sure, they probably hated her now, but . . .

She punched Margo's number.

She could feel herself trembling again.

Surely they would come for her. Help her.

Get her out of here.

"Hello?" Margo's cheerful voice answered the phone.

For a moment, Gina couldn't bring herself to speak.

"HELLO?" Margo tried again. "IS ANYONE THERE?"

"It's me . . ." Gina whispered.

"YES? WHO?" Margo practically shouted. "I

can't hear you. There's too much noise where you're calling from."

"IT'S GINA!" she finally cried out.

She could feel the tears welling up in her eyes. Quickly she turned her face to the wall.

"WHERE ARE YOU?" Margo shouted again.

"At Taylor's," Gina replied as loudly as she could without shouting. "And I want to leave. . . ."

"So go," Margo said flatly. "Leave."

"I . . . I . . . can't," Gina stammered, feeling her chest beginning to heave. "Not by my-self."

"So, what do you want from me?" Margo snapped.

"I was hoping you guys could come get me."

"At Taylor's? Isn't that like a mile away!" Margo cried out. "And why should we, after the way . . ." Suddenly her voice trailed off. Gina could tell she'd covered the mouthpiece and was talking to her friends. Gina's old friends.

The Crowd.

She leaned her head against the wall.

Margo's voice came back on the phone almost a minute later. "Okay. Lewis is going to come get you. Be outside. He'll bring you back here."

"Thanks . . ." Gina whispered.

"But, Gina . . ."

Gina caught her breath. "Yes?"

"Don't expect much," Margo answered bluntly.

Gina nodded and hung up the phone. With her right hand, she grasped the zipper of her jumpsuit and pulled it up.

All the way.

21

Gina plunged through the crowd and headed toward the mountain of coats piled high in the den next to a wood desk. Frantically she pulled at a number of navy wool sleeves until, toward the bottom, she finally arrived at her own.

Quickly she slipped it on and turned toward the door.

She had taken only one step when Lucas appeared in the doorway.

He leaned one hand against the doorjamb, crossed his legs, and smiled. "So. Going somewhere?"

Gina stood in silence before him.

"Too much for you?" he continued. He motioned to the living room.

Gina hesitated. What difference did it make? She was leaving. She'd never go out with him again. She never wanted to. What did it matter?

"Yes," she said softly. "It is."

Lucas nodded. "You need to grow up."

"What's wrong with being thirteen?" Gina blurted out.

For a moment, she froze. The old Gina would never have done that. Never.

Then she wrapped her arms around herself. Why was she trembling again?

Lucas shrugged. "So go already."

Gina nodded once again and brushed past him, into the hallway, out the door, and into the night.

Alexa waited until the words THE END appeared on screen and then promptly grabbed her coat. "Let's go," she said quickly, already sliding through the row toward the open exit door.

"Whoa!" David laughed, catching her arm. "Remember? Stephanie, Julie, and company?"

Alexa nodded. "Oh, who cares about them." She waved her arm in the air as if they were merely particles of dust that could be brushed away.

"Well, I think they're going to be waiting for us in the lobby," David continued. "We can't just walk off."

"Sure we can," Alexa shook her head vehemently. "I do it all the time."

"Yes. Well, I don't," David replied firmly. "Why don't you want to get a soda with them?"

"Because," Alexa replied softly, leaning in toward him, "I'd rather be alone with you."

She watched his face. He wasn't quite buying it.

"Okay," he replied slowly. "But let's just tell them that."

"NO!" Alexa cried out, much louder than she'd intended. "I . . . I . . . mean . . ." she stammered helplessly. What did she mean?

"You mean, you don't want your friends to know we're together, is what you mean?" David finished for her.

"No . . . no . . ." Alexa shook her head.

What was the matter with her? She was usually much faster on her feet. She felt brain-dead.

Not a single good excuse was rearing its beautiful head.

"Okay, then, what is it?" David pressed on. He checked his watch. "It's getting late. I should get you home."

"I . . .I . . ." Alexa looked away.

It was no use. She wanted to be with him. She did.

It was just too risky. Too much to ask.

It required another kind of person.

A braver person. A person who didn't care what others thought.

It was no use. Right now, Alexa was nothing but a crowd pleaser. A very, very tired crowd pleaser.

She thought about Taylor's party. She actually didn't even care what Barry and Gina did. Not anymore. Not a whit.

"You'd better take me home," Alexa sighed

miserably. She turned away, praying he would grab her hand. Confess his undying love, no matter what. Compare her to the sun, the moon, the stars.

But, of course, David did nothing like that.

He was no Romeo.

And she had certainly added up to a very rotten Juliet.

Lewis appeared two minutes after Gina sat down on Taylor's front steps. Tearfully she pulled open the car door and practically flew inside.

"Gee, what happened to you?" Lewis asked. He pulled a bandanna out of his pocket and handed it to her. "I don't know if it's clean."

Sniffling, Gina took it and wiped her face. "I messed up . . ." she began crying again. "With everyone."

"Who's everyone?" Lewis slowly pulled away from the curb.

"Lucas, Margo, Priscilla, you know. Everyone!"

"Lucas who? Baker?" Lewis asked incredulously.

Gina nodded.

"Wow. What were you doing with him? Heck. Lucas is no one to worry about. He blows it with everyone all the time. He's a mess!"

Gina looked up at Lewis through her tears. "What do you mean?"

"I mean, he's messed up at school. He just got kicked off the lacrosse team. He's falling into the toilet."

Gina looked away. "I didn't think so. I heard he was actually kind of nice. That he just had a bad rep."

"Who told you that?"

Gina laughed through her tears. "Someone I shouldn't have listened to." She paused. "Is Margo really mad at me?"

Lewis shrugged. "Something's going on. They had some fight, tryin' to decide if I should bail you out. What did you do? Steal someone's boyfriend? Copy a term paper? What?"

Gina burst into tears again. "No! I didn't! I just . . . I just . . . stopped doing everything they wanted me to do! I used to do it all. Agree with everything. I hate fighting. But then I got tired of always saying YES to everyone. Being so perfect. Reliable. I got sick of it! They were so mean! Always asking for stuff. Always saying, 'Gina can you do this?' 'Gina can you do that?' "

Lewis raised his eyebrows. "Well, did you ever say, 'no'?"

Gina began knotting and unknotting the bandanna. "No." She looked at Lewis. "They'd have probably hated me. Just like they do now."

Lewis suddenly pulled the car over to the curb. He turned and smiled at Gina awkwardly.

"Listen, I'm no wise man or anything," he paused. "But let me just tell you something I figured out a while ago." He shifted in his seat and smiled at her uncomfortably. "People will ask you for whatever they can get. It's the way people are." He shrugged. "It doesn't mean they're bad or anything. Just a little selfish. It's really up to you to say no."

"But they were always asking!" Gina protested tearfully.

"So you still should have said no," Lewis insisted. "I don't think they'd have dumped you. They like you. They'd have just had to get used to you saying forget it. That's all."

Gina leaned back against the car seat. "Well, I did say no. All week. I kept saying I couldn't do this or that. And they do hate me."

Lewis raised his eyebrows. "I heard someone yelling about the awful things you said. What did you say — 'No. Sorry I can't,' or, 'No. Go jump in a lake'?"

Gina giggled in spite of herself.

Lewis turned on the ignition once more. "I thought so." He pulled away from the curb. "Listen, I've got a house full of screaming girls who are getting on my nerves. Straighten this thing out. Okay? It's making me sick."

Gina grimaced. "I'll try. If they'll let me."

Lewis nodded. "Believe me. They'll let you. I'll help."

Gina looked at him curiously. "What are you going to do?"

Lewis smiled. "Hopefully, nothing," he chuckled as he hung a right onto the Warners' street.

They were all there sitting around the table, mounds of cookies before them.

Like a jury on snacktime.

It was sickening.

No one said a word.

Gina looked up at Lewis.

He smiled and glanced around the room. "Someone say something," he suggested. Then he opened the refrigerator door.

Once again, Gina looked around the table.

"You look weird," Vivienne volunteered, popping some popcorn into her mouth. "What's with all the makeup?"

"I never saw that jumpsuit before," Priscilla commented. "It doesn't really look like you. . . ."

Gina bit down hard on her lower lip. Okay. It was time. Absolutely and positively time.

"I think it looks good," she ventured carefully. "I know it's not my usual thing, but I'm sick of always looking so . . . so . . ."

"Collegiate," Lewis offered. "Go on."

"I think it's flattering," Michelle offered. "I do."

"Michelle," Vivienne snapped. "What are you saying?"

"It's the truth. I can be mad at her and still say something nice," Michelle said.

Gina could feel herself relaxing just a little bit. "You do?"

Michelle nodded. "But you made us feel like garbage the other day. What was the matter with you? You're usually so . . . so . . ."

"Agreeable," Lewis volunteered, taking a huge bite out of a ham sandwich.

"Butt out, Lewis," Margo snapped.

"No," Gina insisted. "I want him here."

Lewis shrugged. "She wants me."

Suddenly, everyone started giggling.

"Why did you say those horrible things?" Priscilla continued. "We didn't know you felt that way! You never said anything about it whenever we asked you to do things."

Gina looked down at the floor. "I thought you wouldn't like me as much if I didn't play the part."

"What part?!" all four girls asked in unison.

Gina sighed. "Little miss do what everyone wants, be what everyone wants, say what everyone wants. That's what part."

"But you never seemed to mind anytime we asked. . . ." Vivienne began.

"Actually, that's not true," Michelle said thoughtfully. "Sometimes she said she wasn't sure, or that she really didn't think so . . ." She looked at Gina accusingly. "But you didn't exactly stick to it or anything."

Gina nodded. "I couldn't. I was scared."

"So it's really all your fault," Vivienne proclaimed, looking around the table for support. "You wouldn't speak up."

"Well, maybe . . ." Gina began uncertainly.

"Go jump in a lake," Lewis snapped. "Man, you guys are nuts. You walk around asking her to do this, and that, and a million things you probably wouldn't want to do yourselves, and you don't stop to think how come she's not saying no? It's not all her fault. Give me a break."

Michelle leaned back in her chair. "Well, maybe that's true," she said simply. "I wouldn't want to do so many favors for you guys. No way."

Priscilla pursed her lips thoughtfully. "You know? Me either."

Gina looked around the table utterly shocked. "You wouldn't?"

"NO!" all four girls cried out at the same time.

"Now can we stop this, please?" Vivienne implored. "And, Gina, will you please not get all dolled up like that again? You look, I don't know, weird. Will you look like yourself again? Please?"

Gina took a deep breath. "What's myself?" she asked, looking directly at Viv.

For a moment, Vivienne was stunned. Then she looked at Margo, who turned to Priscilla, who shruggged in Michelle's direction. Then they all looked back at her.

"I . . . I don't know, either," Gina stammered.

She could feel the tears threatening to fall again.

"You're lots of things," Lewis piped up. "I'm a jock most of the time. But I don't always want to wear my sweats. Sometimes I want to look cool. You know. Like a rocker." He shrugged. "I'm an interesting guy."

Margo giggled. "Listen, Lewis. Truthfully, you're a slob."

Gina cocked her head to one side and considered Lewis. "Yeah . . . that's right. That's it. I don't mind looking all neat and clean and collegiate . . . sometimes. But," she looked down at her jumpsuit, "I also want to look like this sometimes. I like it. I feel — " she closed her eyes for a moment, trying to find the right word — "alluring."

"Woo woooooo," Lewis sang out.

"Okay, that's enough out of you," Margo instructed tersely. "Out. The rest is up to us."

Lewis saluted. "Yes, ma'am." And with that, he picked up his sandwich, winked at Gina, and walked out the swinging door.

"One thing," Margo continued. "How did you ever get the nerve to go to that party?"

Gina stared at Margo intently. If she told them, they'd be ready to strangle Alexa. They'd cook up a plan. They'd get her. It was a nice thought. Delicious, really. Except for one thing.

If Gina were going to start sticking up for herself, it was the perfect place to start. She'd let them help another time. That was their way. Just not this time.

"Oh, I don't know," Gina answered slowly. "I guess I was just desperate for a change."

She had to get Alexa on her own. And, actually, she already had an idea how.

After all, she'd believed Alexa once. Twice wasn't much more. . . .

"Well," Priscilla began. She cleared her throat and bowed slightly to Gina. Then she plucked her handpainted jacket off the back of her chair and extended it to her. "Let's see how it looks."

Gina broke into a huge smile and slipped it on.

"Too conservative," Michelle shook her head.

"Maybe we should take you shopping," Margo interjected. "Experiment a little with a whole bunch of looks."

Gina began to blush. "No . . . no . . ." she shook her head without conviction.

"Sorry," Viv piped up, a huge smile on her face. "We won't take no for an answer."

For a moment, nobody said a word.

And then the room was filled with the warm and loving laughter of The Practically Popular Crowd.

22

Alexa stood in the hallway Monday morning outside of her homeroom, fluffing her hair.

This was a new beginning.

Life without David. It had been nothing but misery, anyway. Well, at least part of the time.

"Hi, Alexa," Julie called from two doors down. She waved. "We missed you and David on Saturday. What happened?"

Alexa was ready. She had it all planned.

"Oh, I needed to get home and catch up on some studying." She laughed. "We're not talking a romance here. You realize that, don't you?" She laughed again.

Julie smiled. "Oh. Yes. I guess so." She paused and checked her watch. Hesitantly at first, she started walking toward Alexa. "Ummm, listen . . . I actually wasn't sure you and David were just friends. I mean, Gina . . ."

"Well, we are!" Alexa sang out. "He's really not quite my type." She looked down at her finger-

159

nails. "Terrific guy, though." She smiled at Julie.

It was almost working. She was almost believing her own words. The truth was, David probably wasn't right for her in all kinds of ways. Otherwise, it would have worked.

Alexa frowned. What did this have to do with Gina?

"Well . . ." Julie went on slowly. "I was wondering . . ." She paused and cleared her throat. "I guess you wouldn't care if I wanted to get to know him or anything?"

Alexa froze.

"Hey, Alexa," Julie immediately began to back off. "I won't do it if you . . ."

"But . . . but . . ." Alexa stammered. "You like David?"

Julie grinned. "He's neat. Funny. Cool, really. Lots of people think so. You know . . ."

Alexa nodded. No, she didn't.

Suddenly, she was feeling very sick.

"Hi, Alexa," a familiar voice rang out from behind her.

She whirled around to find Gina Dumont walking toward her.

"How was the movie Saturday night?" Gina asked nicely. "Good, I hope?"

"Yeah . . . yeah . . ." Alexa stammered again, looking from Julie to Gina and back again. This was impossible. She was completely confused.

Julie liked David? Gina wanted to know how the movie was?

It was crazy.

"Well, I just wanted to say" — Gina took a deep breath, her smile slightly less enthusiastic now — "that you are a miserable person." She turned to grin at Julie. "I called David last night. He invited himself along to Leo's later. You're coming, right? He seemed real happy when I told him you were."

"What were you doing calling David?" Alexa snapped.

Gina grinned. "To see how his Saturday evening was. We're friends, you know."

Gina started to walk away, then suddenly stopped. Turning around once more, Gina placed herself directly in front of Alexa.

Her expression was wide-eyed and innocent.

"What was it you said?" Gina paused, as if to think very hard. "Ah, yes." Her smile was triumphant. " 'He's free!' "

Then, with the smile still in place, Gina added, "If you ever do something like that to me again, Alexa, you will pay."

And with a friendly nod at Julie, she walked into her homeroom.

"Was that Gina Dumont?" Julie asked in complete amazement. "Or an alien who just looks like her?"

Alexa ignored the question. "Did Gina tell you

that David was . . . was . . . real popular or something?"

Julie grinned. "Well, like I was trying to tell you, when it seemed like you were seeing him, we all realized he was kind of cute. Especially me. We weren't sure how you felt about him, so we all backed off. But then Gina called me last night and mentioned you told her right out you weren't really interested." She giggled. "I got pretty excited! Especially when she told me he said I was cute. I guess he just wasn't for you. Huh?"

Alexa shrugged wordlessly, bent down to pick up her schoolbooks and, without saying a word, followed Gina inside.

This had to be a bad dream.

No one was acting the way they were supposed to.

Since when was Julie interested in anything but looks?

Since when did Gina act like Rocky and Benedict Arnold all rolled up into one?

Since when did she come out the overall loser?

Alexa took a deep breath.

Since never.

And no one. Not David, not Gina, not anyone, was going to ruin her life. Her star power. Her glow.

Alexa forced a huge smile on her face as she took a seat.

David and Julie sitting in a tree . . .

She couldn't help it.

A single tear traced its way down her cheek and landed softly and silently in her lap.

Alexa gently touched the spot with her fingertip.

A lone tear, for a very lonely, very popular, girl.

Look for the next
Practically Popular Crowd book:
Getting Smart

"Hi!" Rebecca smiled as she looked from girl to girl. "You're all so terrific-looking!" she sang out.

"We try!" Margo giggled as she sucked in her stomach.

"We never thought of ourselves that way!" Gina exclaimed, obviously very pleased.

"You're not bad yourself," Michelle replied. "I love your earrings."

"And we're smart, too," Vivienne offered.

Rebecca grinned at Vivienne. "An A in algebra and cool-looking, too? You're something else. Do you think some of you could rub off on me? Please!?"

Vivienne, all aglow, simply looked around the table at her friends. "I think so. . . . " she said softly.

Priscilla glanced around the same table in bewilderment.

Were they kidding?

Their smiles were so bright. So pleased. So earnest.

Did they really think this girl was for real?

About the Author

MEG F. SCHNEIDER was practically popular when she was growing up in New York City. She remembers feeling very excited and scared, insecure and confident, hurt and happy . . . sometimes all at once! And that is why she created **The Practically Popular Crowd.** She hopes it will help readers understand themselves better.

Ms. Schneider is also the author of the Apple Paperback *The Ghost in the Picture.*

She graduated from Tufts University and received a master's degree in counseling psychology from Columbia University. She lives in Westchester County, New York, with her husband and two young sons.

APPLE® PAPERBACKS

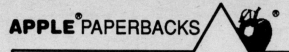

Pick an Apple and Polish Off Some Great Reading!

BEST-SELLING APPLE TITLES

- ❏ MT43944-8 **Afternoon of the Elves** Janet Taylor Lisle $2.75
- ❏ MT43109-9 **Boys Are Yucko** Anna Grossnickle Hines $2.95
- ❏ MT43473-X **The Broccoli Tapes** Jan Slepian $2.95
- ❏ MT42709-1 **Christina's Ghost** Betty Ren Wright $2.75
- ❏ MT43461-6 **The Dollhouse Murders** Betty Ren Wright $2.75
- ❏ MT43444-6 **Ghosts Beneath Our Feet** Betty Ren Wright $2.75
- ❏ MT44351-8 **Help! I'm a Prisoner in the Library** Eth Clifford $2.95
- ❏ MT44567-7 **Leah's Song** Eth Clifford $2.75
- ❏ MT43618-X **Me and Katie (The Pest)** Ann M. Martin $2.95
- ❏ MT41529-8 **My Sister, The Creep** Candice F. Ransom $2.75
- ❏ MT40409-1 **Sixth Grade Secrets** Louis Sachar $2.95
- ❏ MT42882-9 **Sixth Grade Sleepover** Eve Bunting $2.95
- ❏ MT41732-0 **Too Many Murphys** Colleen O'Shaughnessy McKenna $2.75

Available wherever you buy books, or use this order form.

Scholastic Inc., P.O. Box 7502, 2931 East McCarty Street, Jefferson City, MO 65102

Please send me the books I have checked above. I am enclosing $_____ (please add $2.00 to cover shipping and handling). Send check or money order — no cash or C.O.D.s please.

Name _____

Address _____

City_____ State/Zip _____

Please allow four to six weeks for delivery. Offer good in the U.S.A. only. Sorry, mail orders are not available to residents of Canada. Prices subject to change.

APP59

THE *PRACTICALLY* POPULAR CROWD

by Meg F. Schneider

New Series!

It isn't easy being an eighth grader. Meet Margo, Michelle, Gina, Viv, and Priscilla — five girls just trying to fit in and be cool. And with parents who don't understand, fickle boys, and arch-rival Alexa — anything can happen!

❑ BAL45477-3 **Keeping Secrets** **$2.95**

❑ BAL44804-8 **Pretty Enough** **$2.95**

❑ BAL44803-X **Wanting More** **$2.95**

Look for GETTING SMART coming in Summer 1993!

Available wherever you buy books, or use this order form.

Scholastic Inc., P.O. Box 7502, 2931 East McCarty Street, Jefferson City, MO 65102

Please send me the books I have checked above. I am enclosing $_____ (please add $2.00 to cover shipping and handling). Send check or money order — no cash or C.O.D.s please.

Name _____

Address_____

City _____ State/Zip _____

Please allow four to six weeks for delivery. Offer good in the U.S. only. Sorry, mail orders are not available to residents of Canada. Prices subject to change.

PPC692

Get a clue...
Your favorite board game is now a mystery series!

clue™

New Series!

by A.E. Parker

Who killed Mr. Boddy? Was it Mrs. Peacock in the Library with the Revolver? Or Professor Plum in the Ball Room with the Knife? If you like playing the game, you'll love solving the mini-mysteries in these great books!

❑ BAM46110-9 #1 **Who Killed Mr. Boddy?** $2.95
❑ BAM45631-8 #2 **The *Secret* Secret Passage** $2.95
❑ BAM45632-6 #3 **The Case of the Invisible Cat** $2.95
❑ BAM45633-4 #4 **Mystery at the Masked Ball** $2.95

Copyright © 1993 by Waddingtons Games Ltd. All rights reserved. Published by Scholastic Inc., by arrangement with Parker Bros., a divison of Tonka Corp., 1027 Newport Avenue, Pawtucket, RI 02862 CLUE ® is a registered trademark of Waddingtons Games Ltd. for its detective game equipment.

Available wherever you buy books, or use this order form.

Scholastic Inc., P.O. Box 7502, 2931 East McCarty Street, Jefferson City, MO 65102

Please send me the books I have checked above. I am enclosing $_____ (please add $2.00 to cover shipping and handling). Send check or money order -- no cash or C.O.D.s please.

Name _____

Address _____

City _____ State/Zip _____

Please allow four to six weeks for delivery. Offer good in the U.S. only. Sorry, mail orders are not available to residents of Canada. Prices subject to change. CL79